MW00560481

Finders, Inc.

Michael Jasper

Finders, Inc.

http://michaeljasper.net

Cover by Michael Jasper

ISBN: **978-0692309360**

Published by UnWrecked Press
http://unwreckedpress.com

Sign up for the UnWrecked Press Newsletter:
http://bit.ly/UWP-Newsletter

Available from UnWrecked Press

Finders, Inc.
Family, Pack
The All Nations Team
A Gathering of Doorways
Heart's Revenge
The Wannoshay Cycle
The Prodigal Sons
Redemption, Drawing Near
The City of All-Worlds
Unassisted Living
The Last Sorcerer

The Contagious Magic series:
A Sudden Outbreak of Magic
A Wild Epidemic of Magic
A Lasting Cure for Magic

Gunning for the Buddha (stories)
In Maps & Legends (a digital comic with Niki Smith)

Prologue

He hid her away in the basement again.

She rubbed her wrist, wishing her silver bracelet was still there, but she'd left it at home the day before all of this happened. And the last bracelet she'd worn had been a pair of cold handcuffs.

She sank to the smooth cement floor, still holding her wrist and trying not to think about home.

How long had she been here? Two days? Three? She couldn't remember, because this room in the basement had no windows.

It was completely dark, cool, and unforgiving. Like this room had been set up this way on purpose, to hold people captive. There was the main door, which was always locked, and a narrow door on the opposite wall leading to a cramped bathroom with just a toilet and a sink. No light, no mirror. The water from the sink tasted like metal, but she drank it anyway, slurping it up from her cupped hands.

What kind of person, *she kept thinking, had a room like this?*

He'd only touched her twice, this man she'd first seen walking behind her in the mall parking lot.

He touched her once to grab her that first night and shove her into his big SUV with a surprising strength, and a second time tonight to pull her back into the house after she'd tried to escape tonight.

He didn't say much, either. Even when she managed to slip outside tonight and run. Down the sloping yard to the black lake lit up by distant stars and the occasional spotlight of a neighbor's house. She'd run, but she had no idea where she was, so she was immediately lost. And then he'd found her.

She remembered his deadly grip on her arms, followed by a choke hold from behind as she tried to fight. She'd slipped, tearing her shirt and getting mud all over her jeans. But her arms had been too heavy to struggle for long, and her adrenaline buzz had left her too soon. She hadn't eaten much since he'd taken her, so she was worthless in her attempt to escape. She would've killed someone for a bag of Cheetos.

And now here she was, back in the dark, windowless room. Trying not to think, because thinking too hard led to panic. She closed her eyes, clenching and unclenching her empty hands until she relaxed.

Barely five minutes later, she heard his footsteps above her on the hardwood floor, in the nice part of the house. Footsteps growing closer, then pausing at the door leading to the basement. And then he was coming down the basement steps. Coming toward her.

She slid across the cold floor as far as she could into the darkness until she hit the farthest corner, all the while wishing she had something to put in her hand. Some sort of weapon.

She heard the key scratching at the lock, along with the now-familiar jingle of handcuffs. The sounds filled her with dread. She buried her face in her hands, wishing she could hide, but knowing he'd find her.

He'd always *find her.*

Chapter One

Hank Johnson drove up a narrow, almost vertical road south of Boone, North Carolina, at 8:25 on a snowy Wednesday morning in late March.

He needed to pick up his partner Bim in front of Mossy Creek Apartments, which sat halfway up a mountain overlooking Highway 321. The tires of Hank's wheezy old Ford Escort strained for traction on the latest layer of snow as he worked his way up to Bim's place.

And, of course, by the time he'd slid and spun his way to the top of the hill, nobody was waiting for him outside.

Most of the other apartments contained students from nearby Appalachian State—kids half the age of both Hank and Bim—and all of the apartments remained dark in the gray light of early morning.

"*Unbelievable*," Hank exhaled, his breath pluming in a cloud around him. "But not completely unexpected."

He shut off the car, popped open the door, and hurried across the parking lot, leaving the first set of tracks in the newly fallen snow.

Hank stood barely five foot five inches, and he wore chunky black glasses now flecked with bits of melting snow that partially hid his most prominent features: his intense, dark brown eyes. His skin was a few shades darker than his eyes, a trait that had turned heads his way in a curious and sometimes unfriendly way for the past forty years here in this patch of the Blue Ridge Mountains.

He rapped on the metal door leading to Bim's ground-level apartment, switching his weight from one foot to another in his annoyance and anticipation.

After three more rounds of knocking, Hank took a quick look around, checking for potential observers. Then he pulled a piece of wire from his coat and stuck it into the lock to Bim's apartment.

The big man should've given me a key years ago, he thought as he turned the cold metal knob ten seconds later. But that's Bim for you, stubborn as hell.

Hank took one last breath of clean, cold air and pushed his way into Bim's apartment.

The mixed smells of old food, dirty socks, and musty furniture hit him along with a blast of hot, humid air. Hank tiptoed around piles of dirty clothes, crinkled magazines, soda cans, pizza boxes, and a bag of cat litter—Bim had a *cat* now? Hank didn't know that—on his way to the bedroom. A huge new flatscreen TV presided high over the room, its black rectangle of an eye reflecting the mess below it.

Hank had hoped that a couple loud knocks on the bedroom door would be enough, but he ended up having to barge through that door as well.

The heat was even more intense in here, as was the tangle of clutter, but the strangest thing was Bim's soft, high-pitched snoring. It sounded like a huge mosquito buzzing in Hank's ears. But as he stared at the large mound of person buried under a striped black and gold blanket in front of him, he felt a rush of relief. Hank worried that one of these days he'd find his old buddy not snoring, not moving at *all*, after Bim's overworked heart finally gave up on him.

Bim had been big for as long as Hank had known him, and he was now easily over three hundred and fifty pounds. The guy just couldn't stop eating, and he refused to exercise. Hank had long since given up sharing health and fitness tips with Bim, though. It was a losing proposition for someone who only seemed to want to gain.

"Bim," Hank said, poking him softly in the shoulder at first, then harder when he remembered their mission that day. "Wake up, man. Bim!"

Hank remained a safe distance from Bim's bed, reaching out just enough to poke Bim and then retreating in anticipation of what was to come. On about the fifteenth poke, Bim's buzzing snores abruptly stopped. He rolled toward Hank, a big arm swinging hard for Hank's head. Hank felt the breeze from the swing, which missed him by just three inches.

Bim mumbled something that sounded like "Always finder" as he wobbled his way to a seated position in his bed, still barely awake. His light blue eyes were wide in his hairy white face, making him look once more like the chubby first grader Hank had first met so many years ago. Bim groaned and shook his head slowly, still draped in his blanket.

Hank noticed a glint of silver in Bim's left fist that could've been the end of a slim bracelet. He nodded to himself, approving of his partner's dedication to the job at hand. That must have been some dream Bim had been having.

"Frickin' alarm clock," the big guy muttered, looking all of his forty-four years. "Must've stopped working this morning."

"Right," Hank said. He was starting to feel light-headed from the swamp-like aspects of Bim's bedroom. "We've gotta hit the road, partner." He peeked at his watch and winced. "We're a good twenty minutes behind schedule now."

Bim rubbed his puffy eyes, scratched his uneven beard, and made an attempt to pat down his wild, dark brown hair, which was streaked with a good bit of gray these days.

"Was up late last night with Juan, checking out some leads," Bim mumbled.

"Some *leads*. Right."

"Seriously, man. And he found some old Atari cartridges and a console at a yard sale last weekend, so we had to try that out, you know? He had that E.T. game, remember that one? It was so bad and so impossible to beat, we had to keep playing it, you know, until about, um, two a.m. or so..."

Bim trailed off under Hank's non-smiling glare.

"I'm just gonna go get dressed now," Bim said in a meek voice.

Hank stepped out of the bedroom, worked his way out of the messy apartment, and welcomed the cold air from outside.

As he paced around his Escort, not wanting to sit down in it just yet—he'd be doing plenty of that for the next four or five hours on the drive south—Hank mentally pushed away his irritation at Bim. Getting irritated at Bim did no good.

Some people, he thought, just don't have the same high standards for themselves.

He did ten quick deep-knee bends, followed by a dozen jumping jacks.

His current fitness obsession, isometrics, involved lots of stretching, jumping, and muscle-flexing to keep toned. He'd also experimented with cutting back on how much sleep he needed in a day. His goal was just four hours a night. Last night he'd slept for a little over five hours, and he'd followed his short night with a couple big mugs of extra strong coffee.

But with all the flexing and stretching he'd been putting his body through, combined with the lack of sleep, Hank kept battling a nagging feeling that he was *forgetting* something.

He just couldn't put his finger on it yet.

Standing outside in the cold, as more late-winter snow fell silently around him, Hank stretched to touch his toes, blinked his sore and tired eyes, and waited for his partner and his oldest friend to emerge from his smelly and steamy cave.

* * * * *

They departed Boone at three minutes past nine. Bim sat wedged into the unforgiving passenger seat, overflowing into the middle console area, so that Hank had to rub Bim's left love handle whenever he shifted gears. Just as he always did whenever he went on a road trip with Bim, Hank wished his car was an automatic.

For the first hour of the ride down the mountain, he let Bim ramble on about the snow, old missing persons cases, video games, his young and rowdy neighbors at Mossy Creek, problems with the heat in his apartment, the cold, and anything else that came to the big guy's head.

Hank's mind kept rolling from one open case to the next, like the background checks he needed to get set up with Juan for one client, the reports he needed to type up and send to his lawyer buddy in Banner Elk for a couple other cases, and the surveillance he was supposed to be doing for a case that came in two weeks ago. His brain felt too full with all the details he needed to manage back at the office, so getting out on this road trip was a welcome reprieve.

But he still couldn't come up with what he was forgetting, and he did his best not to take out his irritation on Bim. That was another one of his weaknesses, Hank knew. Something else he had to work on in his unending need for self-improvement.

After swallowing hard one last time to make his ears pop on the descent from Boone, Hank glanced over at his old buddy.

Bim was decked out in a slight variation of what Hank thought of as the big guy's standard-issue uniform. No jacket despite temps in the low thirties back home in the mountains. The ever-present dark blue sweat pants. Faded gray T-shirt one size too small for him, the front too faded for anyone to be able to read the jokey, ironic message stretching across Bim's bulging man-boobs. Hank thought the T-shirt once read "Got Lunch?"

And then the flip-flops. *Always* with the dang lime-colored flip-flops, even when the temperature was ten below, with half a foot of snow still stuck to the ground like dried glue. For as long as Hank had known him, Bim had never worn socks.

"Your turn's coming up," Bim said, interrupting Hank's side-eye examination.

At some point Bim had pulled out his new smartphone, a tiny, thin rectangle of blue in his big white bear paw of a hand. He'd been texting with Juan back at the office. Juan would be tracking their progress on one of his own enhanced smartphones, helping them navigate from the relative comfort of their new office building.

As he made the turn, Hank grinned at the thought of the office. He'd bought all the buildings and the land for the Mountain Villa Motor Lodge perched on the southern bluffs of Boone for a song. Sure, the place needed some work, having seen its best years in the '60s and early '70s, but it was going to make a fantastic headquarters for his team.

Juan could set up his servers in his oversized office, and still have space to spread out all his gadgetry and other equipment in the various banquet rooms and dining areas as needed. Marly had taken charge of contacting the various contractors for the fix-up work (the place had been condemned as a hotel when it closed almost two years ago), and she was thrilled to finally have her own office for all of her files and paperwork instead of working out of their cramped little cottage outside of Valle Crucis with Juan.

And Bim had claimed the small, six-sided building outside next to the pool, vowing to work while sunbathing all summer. Hank tried not to let that mental picture invade his brain.

"There you go, 26 South, *mah frien'*," Bim said, slipping into his version of Juan's accent.

Hank made the turn while cringing. Juan barely had an accent, though it became more pronounced when things got heated at the office, or when Marly's mother stopped by. Now *that* woman had an accent. She'd hadn't known more than a dozen words in English when Marly first brought her up here from Mexico over a decade ago.

"You guys are sure about this, right?" he asked Bim. "We don't have time to drive around in circles for the next few days, hoping to bump into April Mae back at the mall."

That was where the white guy in the black baseball cap had nabbed her, outside a mall in Charleston, SC. Security footage had uncovered just two fuzzy images of a man, first walking up to April Mae in the parking lot, then standing right next to her, hands on hips, looking down at her in her car. A tuft of gray hair under his cap. No name yet, but Juan promised they'd have one before they arrived at his place. The footage was from Sunday night, two and a half days ago. Her face had been splashed all over the Internet and news channels on TV since that time, but nobody had any other leads than that.

Hank and his team would find her first. Because with Finders, Inc., everyone comes home safe. It was their unspoken motto.

Bim, meanwhile, hadn't bothered answering Hank's question. He was too busy staring at the roof of the car, at the place where Hank had always wished he'd installed a sun roof.

As Hank watched, Bim's eyes flicked shut; he could've sworn he heard a clicking sound accompany the movement.

He drove on in silence, feeling unsettled. Bim *always* did this, usually at the most inopportune times. Usually whenever Hank had questions for him or if he just wanted to talk. Bim could disappear like this for up to half an hour, and a bomb exploding at his feet wouldn't disturb him. That was Bim for you: never doing the expected thing, and never feeling uncomfortable about it, either.

As they drove farther south and east into the lower flatlands, the snow turned to spitting rain. Hank plowed through the precipitation on the interstate at an even eighty miles an hour, keeping one eye on the radar detector mounted to the left of the wheel, while keeping his other eye on the slowly unfurling digital map on his phone, mounted to the right. The big evergreens and leafless oaks receded, making way for grassy winter fields and empty pasture land wet with mud and the last melting remnants of snow.

He wondered how April Mae had been holding out these past three days. If she was somewhere inside, keeping dry and warm. If she was able to keep a lid on her fear.

Everyone comes home safe.

"Dude."

Hank looked up from the broken white lines of the road, sucking in a sudden breath.

He turned and saw that Bim had ended his study of the ceiling and was now staring at him. He heard a few small jingles of metal from one of Bim's large hands that must have come from the bracelet Bim had taken ownership of, temporarily.

"You doing okay over there?" Bim asked. "Want me to drive for a while?"

"No," Hank said, too quickly. The few times Bim had taken the wheel had resulted in minor disasters, from fender benders to nose dives into ditches. Good thing the old Escort was a tough little car.

"You kinda went away for a while there, bud," Bim said.

Hank laughed.

"Learned it by watching you."

"Whaddaya mean?"

Bim never admitted to spacing off while on a case, but Hank always knew what was going on. The guy was reaching out with his special abilities. *Connecting.*

"Never mind," Hank said. "I was just thinking about all the work waiting for me back home. The usual. What do you guys have for me? I feel like I've been a bit out of the loop on the legwork for this case. These court cases have been eating up all my time."

Not to mention all the texts and phone calls from Mom, he added silently.

She'd set him up on three straight nights of dates, Sunday-Monday-Tuesday, with three different women whose mothers went to the same church as her. Mom was worried about never getting grandbabies, because he had yet to marry, same as his younger brother William (Hank refused to call him "Billy J," no matter how often William asked him to do so). She really wanted those grandbabies.

Hank kept telling her he was too busy running Finders, Inc. and saving peoples' lives, but she didn't seem to get it. William's response was to just disappear years ago. Last Hank had heard, William was bouncing around the country, working odd jobs and eventually getting into some sort of trouble that required an influx of cash from Mom to fix. Which enabled Mom to focus solely on Hank. For *his* love connection, she'd almost worked her way through the whole 35- to 45-year-old segment of the female congregation at her church. Hank feared the 46- to 55-year old segment was next.

He had yet to meet anyone that way who lit a fire in him. Usually, all the dating just made him feel sad—for himself as well as his female counterpart. It felt too much like a desperate competition for some sort of vague, questionable prize.

"Yeah," Bim said after a meaningful pause. "You *have* been a bit outta the loop."

He cleared his throat and glanced at his phone for a second.

"But that's all good, 'cause that's why you have us. Gotta give credit to Juan for finding the neighborhood where this guy lives—he found some emails related to human trafficking coming from a place just outside Charleston, and he was able to compare IP addresses and locate it, all from just one email. That's all the dude needed to crack the case. Now we just have to find where this guy has hidden her and pull her the hell out of there."

"Nice work," Hank said.

He let out a silent sigh of relief as they left the interstate and the sun broke through the clouds for a moment. They'd been in the car for almost three hours, and Hank needed to get out and stretch.

They stopped for a quick fill-up for gas, and Bim volunteered to grab lunch for them both. Hank demurred, but gave Bim the company credit card anyway. He was working on eating just one meal a day, and snacking was for wimps.

While the gas pumped away and Bim flip-flopped his way inside, Hank did some stretches, then knocked out two dozen push-ups to help him ignore the rumbling in his empty belly. He'd gotten used to odd looks from strangers, so he barely noticed the wide eyes in the occasional car rolling past as he got his heart rate up and his muscles burning again.

Bim came back just as the gas clicked off. He watched Hank finish his speed round of calisthenics, grinning and shaking his head.

"Gonna kill yourself exercising all the time like that, Hanky J," he said as he tore open a large bag of Cheetos. He munched on an orange handful as he dropped like a small nuke onto the passenger seat. To his credit, Bim didn't spill a drop of his 32-ounce Coke.

Snacking was for wimps, Hank reminded himself, sniffing the tempting scent of imitation cheese. He dropped into the driver's seat, and they left the convenience store behind.

After they were moving again, closing in on April Mae's location, Hank felt his anticipation growing. And when he started getting worked up like this, he couldn't keep his mouth shut. He needed to talk.

"Human trafficking," he began. "I mean, what kind of term is that? That doesn't even touch on the horror of what's really happening."

Bim shrugged and ate more Cheetos.

"I mean, are we talking *slavery* here? A hundred and fifty years after Abe Lincoln, for crying out loud? It's not right. And a sixteen-year-old girl, too. What kind of sickos are we dealing with here? And in *America*, not some far-off place like Thailand or China. Right here. So messed up."

"I know," Bim said. "Watch your speed here. Drops to fifty-five."

Hank checked the radar detector and maintained his speed of seventy. According to his phone, they were about half an hour away. Very close now. He took a deep breath, held it, and let it out. Forcing himself to stay in control. Always in control.

"So what sense do you have of her? April Mae, that is."

Bim froze, just for moment, with his hand deep in the bag of Cheetos. He pulled his hand out and began licking the orange crud from each sausage-like finger, smacking loudly. Being intentionally annoying in an attempt to change the subject.

"Come on, man," Hank said. "I want to know. You got a touch of her a few minutes ago, didn't you? I saw you holding her bracelet."

"Fine," Bim said, blowing out all his breath and glancing once more at his phone. "Slow down to the frickin' speed limit and I'll tell you. I don't want this bucket to hydroplane and kill us both this close to finding April Mae. I'm worried about this one. I don't like what I saw."

Hank did as he was told, though dropping to fifty-five miles per hour suddenly felt like crawling. He tensed his muscles and chewed his lip some more.

"I saw a jumble of places," Bim began. "The back of an SUV, which was all dark due to the black-tinted windows, and it even had a cage separating the driver's seat from the back seats, like a cop car. Then I saw brown water gushing from a culvert ten feet wide, like a horizontal waterfall churning into a black river, near a busted-up bridge." Bim's voice dropped to a whisper, with a lilt of curiosity to it now. "And the culvert, it was set in these gray rocks, big rocks, most of them jagged and irregular? Her hands were cuffed with cold metal cuffs, but something about those rocks. Sharp rocks all around, I guess? And then, darkness, a room, I think. Cold, no windows."

He felt goosebumps rising on his arms, the skin on the back of his neck prickling as well. Even after all these years of witnessing them firsthand, Bim's skills utterly freaked him out. But he'd never admit that to him.

Bim let out a long belch that made Hank's ears rattle. The car filled with the odor of Cheetos and carbonation.

A culvert, Hank thought. An SUV and some rocks.

"Satisfied?" Bim asked. Hank glanced over at him at last, and saw the big guy's face was red, his wide forehead shiny with sudden sweat. His left hand was clenched into a tight fist around the delicate silver bracelet April Mae's uncle had brought to their new office yesterday. Hank had assured the uncle that they were only borrowing it, and they'd get it back to April Mae soon.

He nodded. He waited a few more heartbeats before saying what had to be said next.

"Try to keep in touch with her as best you can when we get there."

"Dude," Bim said, affronted. "I *got* this. How long we been doing this action together? It's what I do, every time. Except for those few times..."

"I know," Hank said quickly, before Bim started traveling down that long, heartbreaking road. "I figured you did."

He also knew that in Bim's wallet was a business card for Finders, Inc. that had four names written on it.

In the twenty years they'd been working together, the first decade of which it had just been The Bim and Hank Show, they'd only failed to find four people. Bim had written the names on the card himself, in big block letters. He hadn't left room on the back of the card for another name.

Except for those four times, everyone had come home safe. Seventy-one lives recovered; April Mae was going to be number seventy-two.

"The neighborhood's coming up," Bim said, his big hand back in the bag of Cheetos, hunting for the last few orange blobs. Subject officially changed.

Hank elbowed Bim's flab once more as he shifted the car down into third gear. As they slowed, Hank's tension grew.

"So," Bim said with his mouth full. "At what point should we engage the local authorities?"

Hank tapped out a beat on the steering wheel, calculating.

"Not just yet. I have to talk to this guy first. I have to know."

Bim let out another less noisy burp and tossed the now-empty Cheetos bag into the back.

"Hanky J," Bim said in a soft, almost high-pitched voice that made Hank think of his snoring from earlier that morning. "Don't take unnecessary risks, man. Your turn's coming up."

Hank scanned the budding trees on either side of the road, and then he turned left at the fancy eight-foot-high entrance wall made of stones and concrete. The houses here, a good ten miles outside of Charleston, sat on two-acre lots, surrounding a lake that must've been a quarter-mile wide.

Bim's phone beeped.

"Look at that," Bim said, nodding at a house at the end of a driveway almost a hundred feet long, bounded by a treeless front yard with brown grass. He held up his phone, but Hank didn't look away from the house. "Gilbert Menson. Juan got us his name, right on schedule."

The place was three thousand square feet, easy, made of red brick and highlighted with white siding. Two stories, but with a basement peeking out from a hill around the sides. A nice view of the lake from the back deck, Hank could tell.

He turned onto the drive, almost bouncing in his seat now. Bim had taken one last look at his phone, and then he leaned back to stare at the roof of the car again.

They *did* it, Hank thought as the car rolled inevitably forward. Bim and Juan and Marly had brought them right to the guy's house. Gilbert Menson's house.

It never failed to surprise him. Especially when he hadn't had much to do with it, up until this point. Because he'd been too busy, distracted with other—

Wait. He almost had it. Something he was supposed to be doing today. That was what he was forgetting.

But it was too late to follow up on that now. They were officially in the critical portion of this case.

Hank drove right up to the closed garage doors, parking between them so no car inside of it would be able to escape without a ton of damage to both vehicles.

"Lots of privacy out here," he said, whispering now. "No streetlights. No cars in any of the driveways around here."

Bim didn't respond.

Hank killed the engine.

"I'm just going to ask Gilbert for directions," he said, still whispering. "Tell him I'm an old-school traveling salesman who lost his way and is almost out of gas."

"Fine," Bim said in a quiet, somewhat distant voice, still contemplating the ceiling of the car. "She's here. Just... Be careful. You crazy bastard."

"You know me, always careful," Hank said, and then—he couldn't help himself—he gave Bim his wildest "Lethal Weapon" grin this side of Mel Gibson. But Bim wasn't paying him a bit of attention.

Hank popped out of the car without a sound and nearly ran up to the front door. He didn't feel a drop of the cold rain that had begun falling in the past few minutes. He was in the zone now. This was why he did this job: confronting the bad guys, looking them in the eye without blinking, and then taking them *down*.

After flexing the muscles in his arms, abs, and legs one last time, Hank Johnson rose to his full five foot, five inches and pressed the glowing orange circle of Gilbert Menson's doorbell.

Chapter Two

Dark. Dark out here under the half-moon, the night cold and too cloudy for many stars.

The river pulled at her sore eyes through the tinted windshield like a giant magnet. It was a moving creature out there in the darkness, shimmering bits of moonlight reflected in the current. A monster, waiting.

He got out and slammed the front door, yanked open the back. He moved in close to her again, ordering her to get out. She held her cuffed hands out in front of her for balance as he pushed her out of the back seat of his black SUV and onto the rocks. The place smelled like fish and mud.

Legs wobbly, as if she'd been walking all day, or standing without a break, she tumbled and hit her shin on a rock. He'd taken her shoes, not wanting her to run again, and her socks were already wet and muddy.

All she could think about was food. Cheetos. *Hungry. She told herself she was done crying.*

Strong hands gripped her, long fingernails biting into her upper arms. Trying to get her back onto her feet again. She reached out blindly in the dark, grabbed something fist-sized from the ground before rising.

He let go of her arms. He never touched unless he had to. At least so far.

"We all *end up here," he'd said from behind her. Voice low and angry, hint of a southern accent that had never fully faded. "Thrown in once our usefulness is up, washed downriver and carried on out into the ocean to rot.* Remember *that next time you wanna run."*

She was too weak to escape his low voice, and the knowledge both haunted and infuriated her. She made helpless fists, felt something cut into the insides of the fingers of her right hand, and she welcomed the pain.

* * * * *

Bim sucked in a sudden breath, heart hammering in his chest under its thick layers of fat.

I'm not gonna die, he thought as he lowered his gaze from the roof of the tired old Escort.

It was always his first thought after coming back from a connection, especially one where it had been broken. The sound of Hanky J ringing the doorbell had done it for April. She'd been thinking about the events of the previous night again like a kid messing with a partly healed scab. All of the images and words from April Mae's memories had passed through Bim's head in the time it took his fearless partner to get from the car to the front door.

Now he was sweating again, and his mouth tasted like stale cheese and acid. He slid the silver bracelet into the side pocket of his favorite sweat pants with some difficulty in the close quarters of Hanky J's car.

Hanky J. Everyone used to call him that in middle school, but by the end of high school it had become just Hank again. Hanky J had come up with the nickname for himself when they were both twelve, and he'd made a big deal about requesting that folks use it with him. Giving *yourself* your own nickname broke some kind of a rule, Bim always figured, but now he called him Hanky J partly out of habit, and mostly out of stubbornness.

"Wait a minute," he whispered in a thick voice, talking only to himself.

Something was messed up here, something *more* than just the kidnapping and Hanky J's plans to save this girl whose head Bim had been popping into like a mental eavesdropper. Or stalker.

Bim had the sense that Hanky J was walking into a shitstorm. He always did this, playing the lone crusader, going in all by himself. No backup but Bim. And he always told Bim to keep his butt in the car.

We all *end up here.*

Something the kidnapper had said. Just last night, out under the half moon. By the rocks.

The rocks.

Bim sat up straight, slapping his knee and starting a ripple effect on his flabby leg.

That was it. Cutting into her fingers.

I promised Hanky J I wouldn't get involved, Bim reminded himself. Last time I did, we nearly got both our asses shot by that poacher down in the holler close to the Tennessee border.

Bim forced his hand into the tight space between his side belly and the door. He grabbed the handle just as he saw Hanky J disappear into the house.

"*Wait* a minute," he said again as he pulled open the door. Getting out of the car took some effort, because he'd been jammed in there pretty good. Stupid compacts.

At last he made it out of the Escort and onto the driveway, body aching in places he hadn't been able to reach in years. He couldn't stop thinking about the gun tucked under the back of Hanky J's sweater vest. He knew how fast his friend was, though that never made Bim feel any better. Bim's dad had guns, and Dad thought he was good with them, too, just like Hanky J.

He stopped for breath at the bottom of the ten steps leading up to the front door. He had no gun, no weapon of any kind except his own size, which he of course knew was no weapon or shield at all. But he was Hanky J's backup, his partner, and his best friend, so he had to get up those steps and into that house.

He closed his eyes, slid his left hand into his pocket to touch the bracelet, and for an instant he connected to April Mae again.

She was in that room without windows again, still handcuffed, still thinking about how hungry she was. Hungry, and angry.

Her right hand gripped something tight, so tight her fingers ached. The rock she'd found by the river. The one with the sharp, sharp edge on it. She'd already flicked off the light, and she stood next to the hinges of the locked door so she'd be out of sight when anyone opened it.

And someone was coming closer.

Bim inhaled as he came back to his own reality out in the rain, telling himself he wasn't going to die.

Getting up those ten steps took Bim way, way longer than he would ever want to admit to anyone. Hanky J must have picked the lock on the front door and let himself in, because Bim caught a glimpse of him right as Hanky J disappeared down into the basement. Bim tiptoed after him as best he could with his big, lumbering body, his skin prickling like mad from invading someone else's place.

In the foyer, he closed his eyes. He knew he was too slow to get down there to be of any use. It was all happening too fast for him and his plodding self. He didn't even need to touch the bracelet now.

The man was unlocking the door to her room downstairs. She could just barely hear his panicked mutterings. Cracking under the pressure, saying something like, "Can't take it. Gotta go. Too much—"

April's thoughts went black and still in the dark room. Moment of truth time. She wasn't waiting for her rescuers.

In the darkness, she raised the rock.

Bim opened his eyes and clomped down the hall toward the basement steps where Hanky J had disappeared.

They were too late, but not for April Mae Honeycutt.

Downstairs, Hanky J crouched next to a man in a gray sweatshirt who was crumpled onto his side like a balled-up piece of scratch paper. A puddle of red grew around him on his nice hardwood floor. His broken eyeglasses rested two feet from his bloodied head.

Still in the doorway to her room stood a teenaged white girl, barefoot and bedraggled in a torn yellow shirt and mud-caked jeans, smiling madly down at the kidnapper with the rock in her hand, poised for another blow.

April Mae had gone for the temple instead of the throat. Probably a good choice. The dude wasn't moving.

She stepped forward unsteadily, and then Hanky J was up and next to her, taking control of the situation, his small, strong fingers on her wrist, talking low and fast, pulling her away from the kidnapper lying at their feet. Easing the rock from her hand.

Bim stepped down the last few stairs, which creaked angrily under his weight, and he had one last mental connection to April Mae—"Just call me April, damn it!"—Honeycutt.

He didn't need to close his eyes. He just made eye contact with her, and the connection came through.

Another one! The kidnapper's got backup!

Bim felt her sudden fear of him flash through her like a spike of pain, and then he broke the connection as fast as he could. He might have lost his mind otherwise, feeling his thoughts battling with hers at such close range.

He raised his hands in front of him, like a criminal surrendering to the cops. All the while, his face burned and his lifelong sense of shame—tamped down so hard he thought he'd killed it—rose up instinctively, like a whip crack right between his eyes. Just like that, he was the fat five-year-old in kindergarten again.

She had me pegged for a bad guy, he thought, unable to look at Hanky J or April. She thought I was working with her *kidnapper* and not her rescuer. Why? Because I pretty much *look* like a bad guy.

As Hanky J led April away from the room and the kidnapper, Bim pulled out his phone with an unsteady hand and texted Juan and Marly back at the office: "Success! :)"

Then he hit 911 and waited for the dispatcher to start the ball rolling with the local authorities.

As he gave the dispatcher his location and described the situation, Bim gave the kidnapper on the floor a soft kick. He told himself he was just checking to make sure the guy was still alive, but he knew the real reason. From years of experience, he knew what a real bad guy looked like, and what kind of treatment they deserved.

I'm no bad guy, he reminded himself. Then he kicked the unconscious kidnapper a second time anyway.

* * * * *

Before the locals arrived, Hanky J slipped away to check out the kidnapper's computers, leaving Bim and April to wait awkwardly together on the wide front porch. She wrapped herself in an old blanket and sat as far from him as she could, watching the rain roll back in.

He handed her the bracelet, glad to be rid of it, and she accepted it without a word.

"You know," Bim began. He stepped back until he was a good ten feet away from her, feeling large and awkward. "We could wait inside. Out of the rain."

April's eyes went wide, and she gave him that look again. Like he was part of the other team, not the team wearing the white hats.

"I hear ya," Bim said as he lumbered to the far edge of the porch to watch for the authorities. The air seemed a bit cool, but Bim barely felt it. Rain pattered on the roof and dropped onto the grass, never to be seen again.

"My grannie tried to give me a charm bracelet," April said in a soft voice behind him. "It had a volleyball and a music note on it—'cause I used to be on the team and in the band at school—and a heart. I never wore it. Always liked this one better."

Bim heard a sniffle, then another, but he didn't dare move. No way was he even going to say a word and risk setting this poor girl off. And who knew—she might have another rock handy.

Hurry up, Hanky J, he thought as April Mae cried softly on the other side of the porch, her bracelet jingling as she tried to put it back on. Hurry *up*.

Thanks to their past work with identity thieves, Hanky J—with a lot of help from Juan back in the office—was just as nimble with a computer as he was with picking a lock and disarming young women armed with sharp rocks. He wasn't as speedy as Juan, but Bim doubted there was anyone speedier on a computer than Juan. Hanky J's time snooping through Gilbert Menson's electronic files placated Hanky J after not being given a chance to interrogate him, much less even look the guy in the face, thanks to April and her rock.

At last the cops came and whisked away April and her badly wounded kidnapper, and there was about an hour of talk with the local media. Bim tiptoed away from the crowd and did his best to hide out in the passenger seat of Hanky J's Escort. Hanky J loved the media, but Bim preferred the "no comment" route himself.

Long after the sun had set on that long and crazy day, Hanky J and Bim were back in the car and heading north again. It turned out that Gilbert had made plans to sell April to a sex slave ring being operated out of Long Island. He needed the money to get out of the debt he'd been in since he got laid off from his high-tech job three years ago.

Bim kept thinking about what she'd thought when she first saw him come charging into the basement, his long hair and beard all slicked down with rain, belly hanging out of his T-shirt, Cheeto crumbs on his clothes and his green flip-flops. Panting for breath, just from hurrying from the car to the front door to the basement.

As headlights on the highway flashed at them and then disappeared, Hanky J rambled on and on about how this case was going to turn things around for Finders, Inc. The interview he'd done, he was saying, there in front of the kidnapper's house with the local news station could possibly hit tonight's national news.

Staring out the window into the darkness, barely able to see the fattening half moon for all the clouds, Bim realized there was something else he needed to find before he could savor this latest success of theirs.

A couple things, actually. Because if a young girl like April could find the steel in her to take out a man twice her size with just a rock, Bim figured he could muster up the willpower to get his own act together, before all this food he was eating killed him.

He couldn't blame these extra two hundred pounds all on the stress of his job, either. It was something inside of him that always felt hungry, never satisfied. Like a question he'd never been able to answer.

He was going to have to find a way to change, or he was going to die fat, alone, and miserable.

We all end up here, the kidnapper guy had said. Tossed into the river and forgotten.

Bim needed to find a way to change, and it needed to be sooner than later. He never wanted anyone to look at him the way that April Mae Honeycutt had looked at him today, for that terrible second. Never again.

Chapter Three

Shelby hadn't planned on coming back to the nasty no-tell motel today, but she wanted to see the look on the little guy's face when she told him about yesterday. The little guy who was supposed to be her new boss.

Who starts a new employee on a *Wednesday*, anyway? she thought. And then forgets about them?

She gunned the engine to Mom's big old blue Crown Vic to get up the road leading to the former Mountain Villa Motor Lodge. Just like yesterday, the place was in disarray, with the sign off of Meadowview Drive almost done falling over backwards, and both wings of the guest rooms filled with broken windows and scratched-up doors. Dead weeds poked up out of the snow and the pavement everywhere, a clump of them partially obscuring the rusted metal fence around the frozen pool and the six-sided building next to it with its windows opaque with grime.

But the lobby had been clean, she also remembered from yesterday, with a fresh coat of paint applied maybe a day or two earlier from the smell. And the faded, flowery carpeting had been relatively unstained, though a bit dusty.

It could've been worse. She'd been expecting the stink of mildew and dead mice when she walked through the double glass doors of the lobby yesterday, so she'd been pleasantly surprised.

And that hadn't been the *only* surprise of what was supposed to be her first day at Finders, Incorporated.

Just twenty-four hours ago, Shelby had walked through the front doors and took five steps into the lobby, mesmerized by the total silence. This old place had good bones, as Dad would've said. Sturdily built. The floor didn't squeak a bit as she walked deeper inside the wide expanse of the lobby.

Three sets of four armchairs made little islands on the burgundy and blue carpet covering the lobby floor. Shelby guessed the musty smell came from the chairs. Straight in front of her, a half dozen boxes sat on the black reception desk. Guests would've had to walk right under a yellowing and slightly crooked chandelier fifteen feet up and eight feet tall to get to that desk for check-in. Four doors, one in each direction around the lobby walls, opened into what looked like either storage rooms or offices.

Shelby had been about to call out when she smelled gun oil and heard someone breathing behind her and to the right.

"What're *you* doing here?" A female voice, tight with fear and false bravado.

Shelby turned, slowly, and saw a dark-haired, dark-eyed Hispanic woman a few years older than her, holding a small pistol in her right hand. Not pointing it at her, luckily, but holding it at her side, letting Shelby know she had it close. She must have come from the closest office.

"I'm sorry," Shelby began, talking slowly and calmly despite the sudden jolt of adrenaline. She'd been around guns enough in the past few years, so she knew what to do. "I was supposed to meet someone here. Hank Johnson. Black guy with glasses, about yay high? Owner of Finders, Incorporated? But I must have the wrong place."

Something bumped from across the lobby. Shelby wanted to turn toward it, but she kept her gaze on the woman with the gun. The woman glanced across the hall toward the sound and flinched, as if realizing what she was holding in her right hand. She quickly stuffed the gun into the back of her jeans just as a man's voice called out from one of the other offices.

"Marly!"

Shelby risked a look in the direction of the voice and saw a dark-haired man in a black wheelchair roll backwards out of another office as if he'd been shot out of a cannon. He did a smooth turn and focused his intense gaze on Shelby, and then the other woman, Marly. Trying not to stare, Shelby noticed his left leg ended just above the knee, and his right near the top of his thigh. Afghanistan or Iraq vet, she figured. With injuries too high—or too much nerve damage—to allow him to comfortable wear prosthetic legs. As he hurried closer, comprehension filled his face, along with a look of consternation.

"You're Shelby, aren't you?" he said. His chair appeared to be custom-made: it was sleek as a racing bike, and it made no noise as it rolled up to her and stopped on a dime. "I'm so sorry for any confusion. I'm Juan Hernandez, and this is Marly."

Shelby nodded at him and glanced over at Marly, who had taken a step backwards, her face red. To her credit, the woman met Shelby's gaze and gave her a tiny nod.

"Welcome to Finders, Inc.," Juan said, with just a hint of an accent.

She shook his hand, then Marly's.

"*Lo siento,*" Marly said, the words running together. "We've had a couple break-ins already since we starting moving in, mostly students looking for trouble, thinking the place was still abandoned. We've only been here a week now. I found a homeless man in one of the rooms this morning, trying to unpack his stuff and make himself right at home. So when I heard you, I thought he'd come back with friends or reinforcements, and—"

"It's okay," Shelby said as Juan gave Marly a "What the hell did you do?" look. She wasn't going to take offense at the thought that she could've been mistaken for a homeless person. "I'm kinda familiar with guns, you know?"

Marly sucked in a sudden breath. "Hank never *told* me today was your first day."

Shelby figured as much. She shrugged.

"Oh crap," Juan said. He already had his phone up to his ear, probably calling the boss. "He told *me*, on Monday. Right in the middle of moving. I was going to tell you, Marly, but got, ah, sidetracked." He lowered the phone. "And now he's not answering, of course."

"So Hank's... not here," Shelby said, a sentence that had started as a question, but ended as a statement.

She pushed down a growing wave of frustration, tinged with anger at not just the events of today, but the past few months. She *needed* this job, and in this tiny university town, there weren't many good-paying jobs outside of education. No way she was going to cut it as a lecturer. What would she teach? Broken Marriages 101, or Intro to Moving Back Home after 35? *Right.*

"I'm sure this is just an oversight," Juan said, tapping hard on the keys to a slim blue laptop he'd pulled from a black bag on the side of his chair. He spoke with the slightly distracted patience of a tech support guy on a tricky call. "I'll get this straightened out in a minute."

"We've got some coffee over here," Marly said. "Or some water? It's filtered, not the nasty stuff from these old pipes."

"Well..." Shelby began.

I probably won't be staying long, she was about to say.

But then she looked through the smudged glass of the two front doors and saw the small city—more like the big *town*—of Boone spread out below them, its streets lined with snow-tipped trees and light on traffic, with a dozen mountains rising around the bowl of town like silent guardians. This place reminded her of why she'd left the big city, and the view made her feel like a queen overlooking her kingdom.

And really, she thought, where else do I have to be today?

Shelby watched a few cars pass on Highway 321 below them as she inhaled the scents of fresh paint and dust and Marly's perfume. She felt glad not to be in Charlotte right now, sitting in her windowless office at the big insurance agency. Waiting for an interesting investigation to come up, which rarely did. She'd felt like she was *always* waiting for something to happen, either with work or with Wallace. With her life.

"I *could* really use some coffee," she said, feeling a smile slip over her face despite the setbacks of the morning. "Just point me toward the pot. I'll make sure there aren't any homeless folks trying to bum a cup."

Marly let out a nervous laugh at that, while Juan muttered over his laptop.

"Coffee," Marly said, "then the dollar tour. It's the least I could do after what we've already put you through, and you haven't even started *working* here yet. It needs some renovating, but I think you'll like this place."

To her surprise, Shelby had started to agree with her.

* * * * *

She'd stayed around the office for another hour or so yesterday, chatting with Marly and listening to Juan work (and swear in English and Spanish) in his office and the other three offices, where he was trying to set up the computer network, as well as update the software on the various servers, and run cables from one office to another. The guy liked to multi-task.

As it turned out, Juan and Marly were married to one other, and they'd been a part of Finders, Inc. for the past decade or so. They'd been working out of their home up until last week, and they'd been excited to get out (and away from Marly's mother and their kids for a while) so they could actually focus on their work.

Shelby had picked up on Marly's restlessness after the tour of the rundown hotel and her second cup of coffee. She'd seen the stack of about three dozen folders on Marly's otherwise spotless desk, each one flagged with multiple sticky notes. So she'd excused herself, said goodbye to Mr. and Mrs. Hernandez, and attempted to make the half-hour drive back to Mountain City, Tennessee, where she was storing all her stuff and living with Mom. For now. Temporarily.

Of course, her twelve-year-old Highlander had thrown its timing belt on the way back, right before she got to the turn for Skateworld on 421. So she got to spend the rest of her day getting it towed and sitting at Friendship Honda drinking bad coffee and watching daytime TV while they tore apart the engine to her car. Her rebooted life was looking a lot like a blue screen of death.

So today couldn't be much worse, Shelby figured as she threw Mom's huge sedan into Park and let it idle a bit outside the hotel.

She checked out the other cars in the parking lot. Yesterday only one car—a road-salted maroon Subaru SUV—had sat off to the side in front of the right-hand wing of rooms. Juan and Marly's car, no doubt.

Today, three more vehicles had joined the Subaru, all in a line: a white BMW that had somehow managed to stay impeccably clean despite the road grime and snow, a tan-and-brown Ford Bronco that may have been new when Clinton was in his first term, with a faded yellow logo on it, and a dented and dirty green Ford Escort about the same age as the Bronco. The Escort seemed to sag toward the ground on the passenger side.

Interesting, Shelby thought as she warmed her hands in front of the vents one last time. Wonder which car is Hank Johnson's? Bet it's the Beemer. That seems like his style—little man, big-dollar car.

She killed the engine at last and got out. The late-winter wind smacked her in the face, taking her breath away for a moment. She still hadn't gotten used to the cold, even though she'd grown up in this area. In Charlotte, far down the mountain and two hours south, it never got this frigid. She'd forgotten how harsh it could be up here, but Mother Nature was reminding her, that icy witch.

Pulling her coat tight around her, Shelby walked carefully in her new black heels through the snow, wishing she'd pulled on her knee-high boots instead. She had on a variation of what she thought of as her serious work outfit: a dark green sweater that set off her blue eyes and auburn hair—and hid the extra fifteen pounds she'd put on in this stressful past year—and her knee-length black skirt with black tights under the skirt. Despite the winter-weight tights, her toes were wet and freezing from the snow.

I'm not in the big city anymore, she reminded herself as she slipped on the snow of the unshoveled sidewalk. No need to try to play high fashion up here in Boone, in the boonies.

But wearing her best clothes made her feel professional and sharp, and she'd take all the help she could today with her new company. If she stayed on here, that was.

When she finally made it out of the cold and walked into the headquarters of Finders, Inc., utter chaos greeted her.

A small black man with chunky black glasses and a perfectly trimmed goatee stood next to the dusty arm chairs under the chandelier, arms crossed and almost bouncing on the balls of his feet as he talked to a pretty black woman about the same age as him. Shelby didn't recognize the woman, but she did remember Hank Johnson. He was so intent on talking to the woman that he never looked up at the entrance.

Off to their left, a huge white guy with wild dark hair and a scruffy beard, wearing what appeared to be pajamas and stained green flip-flops, was pacing around that half of the lobby. He talked loudly into a cell phone that looked like a child's toy in his huge hand. Shelby swore she could feel each of his footsteps.

Near the back of the lobby, by what was once the check-in area, three men in work boots, jeans, and matching dark blue sweatshirts with a yellow lightning logo were following along after Juan as he shouted directions and complaints at them about the wiring and what needed to be done to fix it to his liking. The men had to hurry to keep up with Juan's speeding chair.

And to Shelby's right, her new friend Marly walked out of her office, took one look at the ruckus in the lobby and promptly stepped back into her office. Her door closed with a slam that Shelby couldn't even hear over all the voices bouncing around the tall ceilings and the chandelier high above it all.

Shelby waved and tried to catch Hank's attention, but the guy remained utterly focused on the woman he was talking to. Probably a customer, or maybe a reporter. Shelby could've turned cartwheels there in the entrance and Hank wouldn't have so much as glanced in her direction.

As the big guy kept on pacing across the carpet to her left, his flip-flops flapping and his huge belly jiggling, Shelby stepped forward and entered the fray. The big guy looked up at her from his intense contemplation of the floor in front of him. His brown eyes went wide for a second, and he froze in mid-pace.

Shelby caught his look and started to say something, but just as quickly as he'd stopped, the big guy did a one-eighty with surprising agility for someone his size. He resumed pacing, still talking into his tiny cell. As if Shelby never existed at all.

She glared at the big guy's back and then checked Marly's door. It remained closed. Just as her gaze was returning to Hank in the middle of the lobby, she noticed an elderly white man sitting calmly on a chair near the reception desk. His gray coat rested on his lap, his white hair perfectly combed. He was an island of calm in the busy lobby. Calm except for the tight fists resting on his bony knees.

Shelby fought the urge to go over and talk to him, reminding herself that she didn't work here, yet. Not in any kind of official capacity.

She dodged a worker unspooling a line of thick blue wire onto the floor and crossed under the chandelier to stand right in Hank Johnson's line of sight. He was talking a mile a minute to the pretty woman across from him, and she held a small recorder in her hand. A reporter.

"The whole team pulled together for this one, really," he was saying. "I can't reveal all the details of our data-gathering, but let's just say the research was substantial."

Shelby caught the quick smirk on the woman's face as Hank rambled on, and then she stepped closer and cleared her throat.

"Hank Johnson," Shelby said. "I'd like a word with you, please."

Hank's head popped up to look at her like it was caught on the end of a fishing line. His mouth dropped open, ending his monologue.

"Ms. *Jamiston*," he said, popping to his feet from his chair in half a second. Behind his spectacles, his brown eyes were wide with surprise. "I am so sorry. You were supposed to start today, and I *completely* forgot it. I knew I was forgetting something," he added quietly, as if to himself.

Shelby glanced at the reporter, who was still smirking, and then she took a calming breath.

"Actually, *yesterday* was the agreed-upon start date, Mr. Johnson. Marly and Juan helped with my, ah, orientation. While you were out."

"Miranda," Hank said to the reporter. "Could I trouble you to wait right here for a few minutes?"

"No problem," Miranda said, turning off her recorder. "I need to talk to Mr. Mayer over there, anyway."

A look of concern passed over Hank's face, just for an instant. Shelby caught it and filed that away for later.

"Oh," Hank said. "Bim? You wanted to talk to *him?* Okay. That's... fine."

Hank looked at all the various people scurrying around the lobby as if for the first time. He raised himself up on the balls of his feet a couple times, rubbing his chin beard. Then he gave Shelby another apologetic look.

"It's not normally like this," he began, pointing at the office back to the left of the main entrance, directly across from Marly's. "Let's head over to my office, and I'll get things fixed up for you."

Shelby had to stretch her long legs to keep up with Hank's short but speedy legs as he hurried across the lobby to his office. He'd just got her set up in a chair in his immaculate but crowded office before he jumped up out of his seat once more.

"One second," the little guy said, and then he disappeared, closing the door behind him.

Shelby sat in stunned silence for a moment. She stared at the eight black filing cabinets that lined two of the walls around Hank's leather chair and his four-foot-wide wooden desk. The top of the desk was cleared off except for a yellow legal pad, a pen, and a tiny blue laptop, closed. No clutter, no framed degrees, no wall of fame. Just right angles and hidden data.

Through the pair of windows overlooking the frozen pool and the town below, snow had started to fall again. And Shelby was *still* waiting.

"*Unbelievable*," Shelby said. She stood up and was in the process of reaching for the pad of paper on top of Hank's desk to scribble out her resignation letter when the door opened behind her. She quickly dropped back down into the chair.

Instead of Hank, though, the big guy with the flip-flops trudged into the office. The room suddenly felt much smaller. Shelby got a whiff of potato chips and Head and Shoulders.

"Hullo," the guy said, out of breath from where he stood next to the desk. "I'm Bim Mayer. Hanky J asked me to talk to you about the company for a few minutes. He apologizes, but he's got a couple fires to put out. I guess."

He held out a big hand for Shelby to shake, and she got up out of her chair to complete the transaction. His hand was warm and his grip was firm, but not crushing.

"Shelby Jamiston," she said. Did he say his name was *Bim*? Really? "I guess Hanky J didn't tell *anyone* else about me starting, did he?"

Bim clumped over to Hank's leather chair and lowered himself into it very carefully. The chair gave one squeak, then surrendered. Bim sighed and shook his head, his long hair flopping from side to side like a wet curtain.

"Nope. Not to me, at least. Don't take it personally. We've—he's—been covered up. You know, really busy. This move here took *way* more effort than any of us ever expected. Plus the cases keep rolling in, and after yesterday, well, you don't even wanna know. But anyway," he added, waving his hand in the air, "that's no matter. Let's talk Finders, Inc."

Shelby didn't say anything for a few long seconds. She was contemplating just walking out, but then she thought about her car in the shop and how badly she needed to get her own place. And she thought about her ex, Wallace, back in Charlotte, who was still trying to find her. How she'd had to leave town in a hurry, with only what she could fit into her Highlander.

"Shelby?" Bim said, scratching his belly through his blue flannel shirt. "You okay?"

Good question, she thought.

"Just wondering," she said instead, giving him a half-smile, "what it takes to get your boss's attention, that's all. This is the second day in a row I've been twiddling my thumbs."

Bim stared at her for a long moment, and Shelby met his gaze. She did her best to give him a poker face, not wanting to reveal that she'd spoken out of turn.

Instead of taking umbrage at her comments, however, Bim let out a loud laugh. Shelby felt the tension in her shoulders disappear at the sound.

"Now *that's* the million dollar question," he said, belly still quivering like Santa's. "That just comes with the territory. Hanky J's got a ton of different things going on, and he's always like that. Totally ADD, but with a good bit of OCD thrown in for good measure. I've known him pretty much all my life, and I don't think he's gonna change now." Bim's smile went away, and he leaned in closer. "But this *is* a good company, and we need some help. Bear with us, huh?"

Shelby nodded, feeling a crooked grin try to sneak onto her face as Bim launched into his spiel about Finders, Incorporated. How they'd started out twenty years ago, just Bim and Hank, doing odd-job private investigations that nobody else in the area would dream of taking on. The first five years had been rough, and they'd nearly given up a dozen times. But each time, right before the money completely dried up, they'd crack open a case, and they'd earn just enough to keep on keeping on. Pretty soon they hit their stride when they focused on missing persons, then they were able to hire Juan and Marly, and things really started to pop.

"Nowadays," Bim finished, "we've got so much friggin' work that we can't keep up. Old Hanky J's been working about eighty hours a week lately."

"Does the guy *sleep*?" Shelby said.

"He aims for four hours a night. Seriously. He read how to do it in a book. But he's not quite there yet. I, um, wouldn't bring that up with him right now. He's a little touchy about it. Sleep dep will do that to ya."

Shelby nodded in agreement at that.

"So that's our sordid little history," Bim said, stifling a yawn. "Sorry. I didn't get *my* eight hours of sleep last night myself."

"So I heard. You two were out finding April Mae Honeycutt last night. Nice work. The media went nuts with her story. Though I only saw Hank—" she couldn't bring herself to call him Hanky J "—on camera."

Bim nodded, but a troubled look flashed over his face. He touched his round belly, just for a second, and then dropped his hand to the desk top.

"Yeah. That girl was a badass. Nearly killed her kidnapper. With a *rock*. Good thing we got there when we did. Hanky J got the situation under control pretty dang fast."

Shelby waited for the rest of the story, including why *Hank* got to take all the credit for finding the lost girl. But Bim had leaned back in the big leather chair dangerously far. He was now staring up at the ceiling, eyes going glossy.

Shelby wanted to look up at the ceiling to see what he was looking at, but she cleared her throat instead. A few seconds later, Bim lowered his gaze and sat up straight again. He didn't glance over at Shelby, nor did he apologize for spacing off.

An awkward silence followed for five seconds, then ten. Gazing down at his hands on his lap, Bim let out a long, slow exhalation.

"So. Who were you talking to earlier, on your cell phone?" Shelby said, uttering the thought an instant after it popped into her head. "Seemed like a pretty intense conversation."

"Oh," Bim said, scratching at the stubble on his cheek. "That was, um, actually, it was my mom. My dad's been kinda sick, and she wanted me to drop by and—well, never mind. Boring personal stuff. You know how it is with parents."

Shelby nodded and gave him a smile, and the worry lines around his blue eyes faded a bit.

"I appreciate you taking the time to chat with me," she said, putting her hands on the arms of her chair, making like she was getting up, hoping Bim would follow her lead. Instead, he just leaned back in Hank's chair, which gave out an ominous creak. "I know you've got a ton of work to do, and I should probably get started on my—"

"*Nah*," Bim said. "I'm in no rush."

Shelby sank back in the chair, intrigued.

"But everyone else looks slam-busy out there."

Bim shrugged. "I'm pretty much just hanging out here in the new digs. Waiting for the next case. My specialty is missing persons. Far as I know, Hanky J doesn't have anyone we need to find right now, so I've got some downtime coming to me. I was thinking about braving the snow and getting a latte and a cinnamon roll, actually, if you care to join me."

As soon as he finished his sentence, Bim's face went bright red.

The big guy was *hitting* on me, Shelby thought with a shiver of delight mixed with dread. She hadn't dated in years. Not since she and Wallace had broken it off for good.

But then an instant later her possibly suitor was smacking himself in the forehead, which didn't do much for her self-esteem.

"Ah man," he said. "I friggin' forgot. My new stupid diet. No more trips to Stick Boy Bakery for scones or sticky buns. Or lattes, for that matter. Ugh. This is gonna *suck*."

This time, Shelby did get up. The roller-coaster conversation with Bim was making her irritable, and she could use some coffee herself. Or bourbon. Definitely bourbon.

"So does 'Hanky J'"—she gave his name air quotes, which made Bim snort laughter—"have a place set up for me? Marly mentioned yesterday that the office across the way from this one was open."

"Go ahead and claim it," Bim said. "That's the big thing to remember here. You have to just take the initiative on stuff like that. Hanky J doesn't sweat the small stuff. He's a good boss, though, and he helps a crapload of people." He finally got the hint and, with some groaning effort, he stood up as well. "Let's go get you set up over there. Hopefully Hanky J and Miranda from the high-and-mighty *Charlotte Observer* have finished their pissing contest by now."

Shelby followed Bim out of the office, feeling a bit taken aback by the immensity of the guy. He was like a boulder with legs. The sides of both his upper arms brushed against the door frame, making Shelby less concerned about her own curves as she walked through the doorway with plenty of clearance on either side of her.

The lobby had quieted down quite a bit in the past half hour, but Hank and the reporter named Miranda were still deep in conversation under the chandelier. Juan had made sure the electricians were set up and working in the space behind the black reception desk, while he was typing furiously on his laptop outside the door to his office. She could just catch a glimpse of Marly, bent over a pile of paperwork in her own office and talking into a phone at the same time.

Shelby saw the old white man still sitting in the hall outside Marly's office, and she was about to point him out to Bim, when a bothersome thought hit her.

"Bim," she called out before he could start crossing the lobby to the fourth office. He stopped and turned, rubbing his belly absently as if it had been growling. "I'm not taking this office from *you*, am I?"

He let out another snorting laugh. Shelby kind of liked the sound of that laugh, as potentially obnoxious as it might be at times.

"Hell no. I don't need an office for what I do. I mostly hang out at home, get caught up on movies and video games, and wait for Hank to pick me up and go find someone. I'm not really a paperwork-and-phone-call kinda person, y'know?"

Shelby nodded, not understanding at *all* what Bim's job description was beyond simply finding people. She was intrigued now.

As she and Bim passed by Hank and Miranda on their way to her new office, Shelby's new boss looked her way at last.

"Five more minutes," he said to Shelby, giving her a quick thumbs-up. "We're almost done here."

Shelby nodded, wishing for an apology in there somewhere, but then her wishes were interrupted by the sounds of sparks and swearing.

The commotion came from one of the construction workers behind the reception desk. Juan sped in to pull the guy away from the explosion of electricity pouring from the bad wiring spilling out of an outlet, just as the other two electrical workers came running up from down the hall. Soon all three workers and Juan were cussing and yelling, in English and Spanish.

Meanwhile, the old man in the light blue suit who'd been sitting outside Marly's office stood up and began clapping his hands as loud as he could.

"*Excuse me*," the old man called out, not looking at anyone in particular. He stopped clapping in the sudden silence he'd created in the office.

Everyone had turned his way, including Juan and the electricians. Even Marly had stepped away from her desk to peek out of her office.

"Excuse me," he said again in his shaky old man's voice. As he spoke, his voice increased in confidence and volume. "I came here for some help, and I cannot wait *any* longer!"

He cleared his throat and looked directly at Shelby. He gave a dramatic pause, convincing Shelby that he had to be a professor, most likely liberal arts.

The blown electrical outlet behind Reception gave one final, sizzling pop, as if trying to get in the last word.

Shelby caught herself trying again to grin despite all the frustrations of the past day and a half. In that moment, she was glad that she was here today to be a part of this barely controlled chaos.

"I am *missing*," the old man said, enunciating carefully, "my car, my dog, and my wife, and I need you people to *find* them *all*!"

Chapter Four

Today was supposed to be our victory lap, Hank thought as he pushed past Bim, Marly, and a pair of electricians on his way through the lobby toward the upset old man. But it's turning into a great big pile-up instead.

He elbowed the third electrician in the belly and boxed out against Bim so he could get around Juan's wheelchair, but by the time he got across the lobby to the mildewy hallway, the old man was gone. Hank looked up in time to see the door to the fourth, unclaimed office close behind the old guy and Shelby Jamiston.

"Oh no you don't," he muttered. "Not in my house."

The new hire had done the right thing and moved the old fellow quickly out of the fray and into someplace quiet so they could talk. Hank approved of her fast thinking, but there was no way he was going to get scooped by her. She hadn't even been trained yet.

He headed to the closed office door, ready to leave the crowded lobby behind. At last people were starting to disperse and head back to their other work.

"*Johnson*," Miranda called from under the chandelier.

Hank felt his shoulders clench. When he stopped and turned, the office went completely silent, everyone watching him and Miranda. Nobody looked at them directly except for Bim, who let out an amused chuckle from next to the reception desk.

"Get to work, y'all," Hank said, and that broke the spell. Everyone moved away, reluctantly.

"I forgot to give you this," Miranda said. She held out her business card, but before he could take it, she turned it over so he was sure to see the number written on the back. "My private number. Tell *your* mom to tell *my* mom that we're going out Friday night in Charlotte. Someplace *nice*, Johnson."

He bit back his almost-automatic response of "Call me Hanky J." Instead, he gave her a smile that probably looked pretty fake, and then he nodded at her.

"I gotta take care of this. I'll give you buzz later. Great chatting with you again. Let us know when the story will run."

"Oh I will," Miranda said from over her shoulder, already heading back out into the cold and snow.

Hank didn't dare look over at Bim. He'd never hear the end of it if he paused now, freezing up like an unmarried forty-something caught in headlights. He really wished Mom would've *told* him about Miranda's divorce at some point in the past year or two. The girl still had it in the brains and the looks department, even if she still pushed all of Hank's competitive—and insecurity—buttons. Some would say those were the same button.

He took a deep breath and remembered the frail sound of the old man's voice, and how it had cut through the commotion in the headquarters like a scissors. His car, his dog, his wife. His *life*.

Everyone comes home safe, Hank thought, doing his best to forget about the mischievous look in Miranda's light brown eyes so he could focus on the task at hand.

He knocked once on the office door and stepped inside.

"...And here's my most recent picture of her," the old man said, holding up a surprisingly new and ridiculously large smartphone with an unsteady, liver-spotted hand. He and Shelby sat side-by-side on the two metal folding chairs in the small office, ignoring the second-hand desk near the back wall altogether. Hank entered at just the right moment to snag the phone from the old man's hand before Shelby could.

Always with the perfect timing, he thought.

"Lovely lady," Hank said after a glance at the smiling elderly woman with long white hair in the photo. She was holding a drugged-looking Jack Russell terrier that also appeared to be smiling.

He maneuvered smoothly between the two of them, aiming for the desk. On the way, he passed Shelby the unwieldy phone and ignored the annoyed look she was giving him for interrupting. He rested his rear against the desk and looked out at his small audience.

"I apologize for the long wait, sir. My name's Henry Johnson, and I'm the owner of Finders, Inc. I see you've already met Ms. Jamiston, who's one of our most experienced investigators."

He and the old man shook hands, and when he caught Shelby's eye-roll at his description of her, he had a hunch that he'd hired the right person for the job.

"James Holhouser," the old man said.

Hank let go of his hand and blinked. The name rang a bell. Hank's brain did some quick retrievals.

"The sixty-eighth governor of North Carolina? From '73 to '77? But I thought he'd…"

"Yes," James said with the hint of a smile. "He passed last year. My last name is *Hol*houser, not *Hols*houser. Just one S."

Hank grinned at that, liking James a bit more now.

"I'm sure you get that a lot," Shelby said, leaning closer to hand him his phone back. "Your wife Delia is lovely. We'll find her very soon, James."

Hank had to work a bit to make it up there, but he managed to perch himself on top of the tall desk. He decided to let Shelby carry on the interview. To her credit, she didn't once look over at him for permission or assistance. She saw her opening, and she jumped right in.

"You last saw her Monday afternoon around one p.m.," she said, "and you went to the police *yesterday* around five p.m., correct?"

Why the long wait? Hank wanted to jump in and ask.

"And you waited for *over* two days because…?" Shelby said, not missing a beat.

"We don't currently, ah, live together," James said. He gave Shelby an embarrassed glance. "She still lives at home."

Hank looked closer at the old man. His suit was slightly wrinkled, which was understandable, but the dark blue paisley tie James wore had been tied over what looked a lot like a silky blue pajama top.

You sly old dog, Hank thought with a grin. You busted out of the nursing home to come here!

"We both used to teach at the college," James continued, talking quickly now before he had to answer any possibly incriminating questions, no doubt. "I was Comparative Literature—" Shelby nodded quickly to herself, as if confirming some minor mystery in her mind about James "—while my Delia was Chemistry. Organic and Biological. I guess it shows that opposites attract."

Shelby smiled at that and nodded for him to continue. Neither of them paid any attention to Hank, which suited him just fine.

"We've been together over fifty years now. Retired from teaching for ten. We'd been talking about moving south, to Florida with all the other white-hairs, but we just can't seem to leave, even with these winters. It's the prettiest place in the world, Delia always said. And I agree."

"And Delia never mentioned a trip or a quick visit with family she was planning on taking?"

"No. She mostly keeps to herself these day, reading and keeping up with friends and family on Facebook. Especially in the winter, when most of our friends are off somewhere warmer. Delia hates driving in the snow."

"No last-minute trips to see a son or daughter?" Shelby asked.

"We never had kids. Never had..."

James abruptly put his hand on his chin, as if thinking over his response, amending it on the fly. His watery blue eyes went out of focus.

Hank felt a chill run down his back. The old guy's sudden blank gaze reminded him of the way Bim would just space off when he was connecting with someone they were trying to find.

Then James closed his eyes, and he let out a soft snore.

"James?" Shelby reached out for him, but stopped an inch from his shoulder. She shot Hank a quick look as if to say "What the heck?"

"*Wait*," Hank said. "Don't touch him."

"What? Why?"

Before Hank could respond, James jerked his head up with a sudden snort, knocking his perfect white hair out of alignment. His eyes opened and went wide.

"What's going on here?" he said in a voice that started out demanding and ended with a trill of fear in it. "Who *are* you two people?"

He gave Hank an especially long glare, and then he turned back to Shelby, his lower lip quivering.

"I don't like the looks of that fellow," he whispered to her in a confidential tone. "Reminds of this thug fellow I met the other day..."

Hank fought the urge to jump off the desk and get in the old guy's face for that. He managed, but barely.

"It's okay, Mr. Holshouser," Shelby said. "We're friends. You were just telling us about your recent problem. With your wife, *Delia*."

The clouded look on his face continued up until he heard his wife's name. Then his eyes cleared with a quick blink.

"It's Holhouser, just one S. And I'd like to *see* Delia again," he added in a sad voice that threatened to break Hank's heart, despite the dirty look James had given him a moment ago. "Do you think you could set up a visit for her here? She doesn't drive much, but we could arrange a car or taxi to pick her up. I have an old friend who runs a fine taxi service. I believe it's the only one in town, but it still has great rates. He gave me a lift here this morning, actually."

Hank nodded. He'd been wondering how James had made it here after slipping away from the home.

"We'll find her for you," Hank said.

"We should start by looking over things at your home," Shelby said. She patted James once on the shoulder, as if relieved he was back with them, but not wanting to get too close to the old fellow and spook him.

James coughed once, the noise surprisingly loud in the small office. He cleared his throat and stood up. Hank wondered if he was wearing pajama pants under his dress slacks.

"Let's go," James said. "I'll show you the way, so long as you drive. I haven't had a license in six years."

Hank noticed with a flash of irritation that James was talking to *Shelby*, not him. But the old fellow was completely aware again, no longer confused.

"Let me introduce you to my partner," Hank said, hopping down from the desktop to once again interject himself between client and co-worker. "His name is Bim, and his specialty is locating people."

He leaned in close to Shelby, catching a nice whiff of her mixed scents of orchids and coffee, and got up on his tiptoes to whisper in her ear: "There are half a dozen nursing homes in the area. Get with Marly and find out where James is supposed to be, and tell them we'll get him back safe and sound. Don't need any Silver Alerts going off while we're at his house."

"Yeah, but..." Shelby began.

Hank had popped ahead of her to open the office door so he could hurry James out into the hall ahead of her.

"We'll take it from here, Shelby," he said. "Thanks for containing the situation earlier, and for getting him settled down. Nice work."

He scurried out of the office before Shelby could say anything more. He didn't mind facing off against kidnappers or armed felons-to-be, but dealing with an angry woman made him want to run off like a pre-teen caught playing doctor at the neighbors' house.

No wonder I'm not married at my age, he thought.

He found Bim kicked back in the arm chair that Miranda had been sitting in earlier, during the interview. The big guy was fiddling with something on his phone, his fat fingers moving faster than Hank had ever seen the rest of Bim move. The front legs of the chair lifted off the ground as he abruptly leaned back in the shuddering chair.

"Bim," Hank said, just as Bim sucked in a quick breath and bellowed "Juan!" at the top of his lungs.

"Oh my," James muttered in a soft voice next to Hank. "That's a large and loud fellow."

"Bim," Hank said again.

"The wireless still ain't picking up jack, man! Can you boost the signal or something? Come on! I was watching something out here on my phone, then it crapped out, and now I gotta—"

"Bim!" Hank shouted.

Still tipped back, the big guy jumped at the sound of Hank's and started to topple over backwards in his chair.

But Hank had been expecting that, and he closed the distance between him and Bim in time to push Bim and the chair forward onto all four legs. It wasn't until a few seconds later that Hank became aware of how close he'd come to being crushed under Bim and the chair.

All in a day's work, he thought, giving a sheepish smile to his new client, who was still gawking at Bim quivering to a rest in the chair.

"This is Mr. James Holhouser," Hank told Bim, waiting for his partner to stand up and be polite. But politeness was a concept that Bim Mayer had never concerned himself with much. Hank blamed Bim's father for that. "You probably heard him mention earlier what he was missing. We're going to drop by his house."

"Have fun," Bim said, his gaze sucked back to his tiny phone.

Hank kicked him right in the flip-flop, hoping James didn't see it.

"Get your coat," Hank said. "And quit joking around, *buddy*."

Bim gave Hank a long, heavy-lidded look, as if he was about to start his usual brand of trouble, but then his gaze caught James behind Hank. Without another word, Bim worked himself up out of his chair. The process took quite a few seconds.

And then, wearing just a faded black Faith No More T-shirt, gray sweats, and green flip-flops, Bim led Hank and James Holhouser out into the cold.

* * * * *

"That's an *excellent* question," Hank said to James, who sat in the middle of the Escort's back seat. No way Bim was going to fit back there. "I guess I owe it to my dad for getting me interested in helping people and making sure folks adhere to the law. He was a police—"

Bim interrupted with a loud whistle.

"Nice neighborhood, Mr. Holhouser. I guess professors do pretty well, huh?"

Hank cleared his throat in frustration, aiming the noise at Bim. They were about five miles from the office, heading north and nearly straight up into a pricey neighborhood with a great view overlooking the town and the university at its northern boundary.

"We saved and lived frugally," James said in an almost absent way. "And we bought it cheap, back in the '70s, when the neighborhood was new, and..."

Hank glanced at him in his rearview, wondering if the old guy was about to drift off to sleep again.

No wonder he spent the morning so quietly on that chair outside Marly's office, he thought. He was probably napping at least half the time.

But James was now awake and leaning forward.

"We followed the *rules*," he said, tapping on the back of Hank's seat with each word. "And look at what happened to us. Something bad has happened to her."

"Can't think that way," Hank said as he turned up Lady Slipper Lane. He bounced his right hand off Bim's side-belly when he shifted into second. The Escort whined in response and inched up the steep drive. "It's the rules and the laws that keep us separate from the animals."

"And the terrorists," Bim added with a scoffing noise. "Don't forget the terrorists who hate America."

"I'm serious," Hank said, glancing once again at James. "This will all turn out to be some kind of misunderstanding. Most situations like this end up that way, with everyone having a good laugh at bad communication."

Bim made a quiet grunt at that, which Hank also ignored.

"There's my house," James said, then added in a brighter voice, "and the living room light is on!"

"There you go," Hank said. He pulled onto a paved driveway that lead to a handsome white ranch house with a perfectly manicured lawn peppered with a dozen maple trees. "She's probably the one looking for *you*, James."

But when they got to the house, the doors were all locked, and nobody answered the doorbell or their knocks. James let out a long, shaky sigh.

"Do it," Bim said in a low voice, tapping the black-painted doorknob attached the front door. "I'll distract Gramps for ya."

As Bim placed his large self between him and their client, Hank pulled out his lock-picking tools and slid a pair of wires into the keyhole for the front door. A twist, a pull, and a click, and the doorknob turned for him.

"Okay, James," Hank called out. "Looks like the door wasn't locked, after all. Stay close as you show us around, okay? We don't need to get split up."

Hank didn't say anything beyond that, including the fact that someone unsavory might still be inside, looking for trouble. You never knew.

"Oh," James said, a single syllable that was full of a dozen questions and fears.

Hank went in first, and then Bim flip-flopped inside after him.

"Bim," Hank whispered before James could follow them in. "Let's try to find a couple of Delia's things to take with you, in case she's not sitting in the bath with classical music playing on her headphones."

"Roger that."

"And be careful. I don't think anyone's here, but..." Hank patted his lower back through his coat, where he kept his gun.

"Right."

Finally, Hank let James into the house, and the old guy smiled sadly at his former home.

"How about your dog?" Hank asked the old man as his listened to Bim shuffle around the house, making the floorboards squeak.

"Oh, *that*," James said. His face grew red. "I forgot that we let the neighbor boy have him when I moved into the home a while back. It just sort of slipped out, I guess. Years of teaching twenty-year-olds will make you say things like that, just for effect. To get your attention."

"Right," Hank said. "Probably a good thing the dog's not lost. We're not so great at finding animals. Not our specialty."

They went slowly, room by room, and James made note of small things that had changed since he'd moved out: a new picture on the wall, a crack in a tile, a window hazy with age. Hank kept track of them all, but nothing jumped out at him until they hit the master bedroom. Most of Delia's clothes were gone from the dresser, though all her dress clothes remained in the closet. James thought a couple pairs of her shoes were gone as well, but the woman must've had three dozen pairs still lined up on the floor of the closet.

Hank slid open the top-most dresser drawer and, with his back to James, grabbed a pair of earrings and a pen cap from inside without a sound. He turned back to his client with the objects hidden in his hand.

"Looks like she went on a trip," he said carefully, not wanting to upset James further. "Like she threw together some comfy clothes and hit the road."

"But she didn't *tell* me. I don't understand."

Bim poked his head into the bedroom. "I think I understand," he said with a lascivious wink.

"What do..." James began, and then he stopped. He began shaking his head back and forth. "No, not my Delia..."

"Delia's gone, hmm hmm, Delia's gone," Bim half-sung, half-muttered.

"Bim," Hank said. "Go out to the car. Now."

"I hate that song," James said in a soft voice. He began checking the other drawers in the dresser, then moved to the master bathroom.

Hank put a hand on Bim's rounded back and pushed him out of the master bedroom. He pushed the earrings and the pen cap into Bim's big palm.

"*Go*," he said as loudly as he dared.

"What? What'd I do?"

"You're not helping right now," Hank said. "Don't be part of the damn problem. Go do what you do best. On your own."

Without another word, Bim stomped down the hall as loudly as he could in his flip-flops. He left the house, slamming the door on his way out. Hank felt a chill breeze slip into the otherwise warm and cozy ranch with his buddy's departure.

"All her medicine is gone, too," James said as he stepped back out of the bathroom. "Maybe she *is* stepping out on me."

"Sorry about my partner's behavior," he said to James, ignoring James' theory. For now. "Bim doesn't get out much."

As Hank got closer to him, he could see that the old guy's face was white, and he looked like he could use a sit-down before he fell down.

"Quite all right," James muttered. "He appears to be a difficult fellow to work with. He must have some significant skills, I'll bet. To make it worth keeping him around."

Hank nodded slowly at that, thinking not of Bim and his terrible way with clients, but of his own personal code. Their talk with James on the drive up here had got him thinking about them again. Maybe it was him mentioning Dad in answer to one of James' questions. A question that Bim hadn't let him finish, surprise, surprise.

In any case, Hank had three simple rules that guided him in his life. He thought of them as his Three Do Nots:

Do not kill.

Do not compromise my beliefs.

Do not let my emotions get in the way.

He'd shared these with only one other person—Bim—and that had turned out to be a mistake. It had been early on, in the second or third year of Finders, Inc., and they'd been struggling to keep things afloat. Bim had laughed and said, "Good luck with *that*."

"Which one?" Hank had said, regretting his confession already.

"*All* of 'em, dude. You're in the wrong line of work for that kind of thinking."

Shaking his head at the memory, Hank let James lead him out of the bedroom so they could do one last pass of the house. Not only did he need Bim out of the house so he could focus—and keep Bim from further upsetting their client—but he wanted to give Bim some time with Delia's personal items to see if the big guy could establish a connection.

Hank wasn't clear on *why* Bim's ability worked the way it did, but over time he'd come to not only trust Bim's methods, but to rely on them. Hank *might* have been able to find all those folks in the past two decades on his own, with the excellent help that Juan and Marly gave him, but having Bim working on his side had definitely saved Hank tons of leg work. But most of all, Bim had saved *time*, which in these cases, often meant saving lives. They had been able to help dozens more people as a result of his skills.

All the big guy needed was a few items that had belonged to the missing person. With those items, and some key facts about the absent one, Bim could usually make a very rough initial connection. Sometimes that was enough to located the lost person.

"You think something bad has happened to her, don't you?" James said from behind him.

Hank had been staring out the kitchen window at the Holhouser's oval back yard and brick patio, which were bounded by more tall maples. Everything was still covered in snow, and no footsteps had broken up the inch of white stuff on the yard and patio. A set of wind chimes tinkled in the breeze from their perch on the end of a black shepherd's hook. The scene was peaceful and strangely lonely to Hank. Like this little patch of privacy hadn't been used in a long time.

"I try not to think that way, ever," he said to James at last. The old man had moved next to him to gaze out at the back yard as well. "Once you start heading down that road, it's hard to turn back."

He put his hands on the cool marble of the kitchen counter and pushed himself away before he got too philosophical. Probably too late for that, he thought.

"This is just one of those detours that life throws at you," Hank said, and he caught the quick smile James made at his extended metaphor. "You have to sit through the work delays and bumpy bits of road and know that when you get to the end of it, you'll be in a better place."

"Well said," James murmured. They walked out of the kitchen and into the front room. He patted Hank on the back with a shaky hand. "I knew I'd come to the right place this morning, after the cops gave me the brush-off. Something about your company just... felt right."

Hank swallowed his knee-jerk reaction, which was to downplay James' confidence in him and be all humble. But that wasn't what James needed right now. He simply nodded back at him and opened the door leading outside for him. Hank left the same light on that had been on when they arrived. It was time to go.

And let's just hope, Hank thought as they left the house and he pulled the locked door shut behind them, that this little detour doesn't end up in a car wreck after all.

Chapter Five

Shelby had to close the door to her new office and be alone for five minutes after Hank hustled James Holhouser—*just one S!*—and the big guy Bim out the front doors and into the snow that morning. She'd flicked off the light, stretched out on her back on the thinly carpeted floor, and tried to meditate to clear the frustration filling her head and limbs like a toxin. There wasn't anything else for her to do at that moment, anyway, because Hank had taken away her resources for this case and stolen all of her avenues for gathering evidence.

But she had too many thoughts swirling through her head that morning to even try to make them stop with a little deep breathing.

Where might Delia be? Did she just run off for a quick trip with a friend, or possibly a lover? What was making James lose his focus and doze off like that, and did that have anything to do with his wife going missing? How can I get this case back so I can solve it?

She had so many questions, but none of them had to do with the issue of whether she was going to *continue* working at Finders, Inc. At some point during her chat with James she had decided this was the place for her, even with the strange way her new boss ran his company. Shelby was hooked.

And, she thought, there's no time to lie on the floor, staring up at the ceiling in the dark.

She rolled up into a sitting position, then got to her feet with a sudden rush of blood to her brain. Feeling unexpectedly refreshed, she let those nagging questions and concerns propel her out of her new office and towards Marly's.

I've got *plenty* of resources, she thought with a relieved chuckle, and lots of avenues for gathering evidence right here in this office. Time to put them to work.

She noted that the electricians had packed up and left, and Juan was back in his office attacking a keyboard like it had just insulted him. Marly was talking in a low voice to someone on the phone about a logo and a sign as Shelby passed by her office. The calm of the office now threatened to lull Shelby into a false sense of security, so she grabbed another cup of coffee to keep the edge on. The stuff tasted like tar, but it was hot, and it did the job all too well.

Marly had just ended her call when Shelby knocked on the door frame to her office.

"Another reporter," Marly said, tapping the phone and shaking her head.

Shelby raised an eyebrow, wondering why Marly would be talking to a reporter about a logo, but she let it go.

"He wanted to talk to Hank about the April Mae case. Bunch of ambulance chasers. That case was so yesterday. Literally."

Shelby had been following April's case from the start. She'd wanted to talk to Hank and Bim about how they'd managed to *find* that girl when so many others had failed. None of the stories about the case she'd read last night and this morning had shed a bit of light on their process, and she imagined Hank preferred it that way. She hoped the reward money from finding April Mae—last she heard it was five figures—would go toward more renovations of this place. And maybe some employee bonuses, too, while they were at it.

"It *was* a pretty amazing rescue," she said in a neutral tone of voice. "You guys did great work."

Marly's motioned for Shelby to take a seat. Her office had folding chairs as well, but Marly's chairs had cushions on them.

"Thanks. Juan put in a lot of overtime on that one. We gotta get him to show you how he pulls data together sometime." She put a hand up next to her mouth, as if whispering confidential information. "Most of it probably isn't legal, but he's got a ton of safeguards in place. He probably put in more time than Bim and Hank combined. But they're the ones out there facing down the bad guys, while Juan and I are here, safe in the office, doing the behind-the-scenes work. It all balances out."

Shelby nodded, wondering how long Marly had wanted to be a private investigator instead of an office manager. It was obvious from the look on her face as she discussed finding April Mae. She could ask her, but Shelby doubted Marly would take it well, being as Shelby now had the job that Marly wanted—and most likely thought she deserved. So she tried a different approach.

"Is that how these investigations usually work? Just Hank and Bim out there, pounding the pavement?"

Marly nodded as her hands drifted over to the piles of files spread out over her desk, which was a twin to the desk in Shelby's new office. Some files were overflowing with paperwork, while others looked almost empty and untouched. Without even looking down at what she was doing while they talked, Marly had been straightening the pages, photos, receipts, newspaper clippings, and photocopies in each file, setting the cleaned-up files in a neat pile on her right-hand side, next to her closed black laptop.

"They've got this good-cop, fat-cop thing going," Marly said, and was about to say something else when she realized what she'd said. Shelby cracked up both at her comment and her look of sheer shock. A moment later, Marly laughed along with her.

"I didn't mean it that way," she said, rubbing her face and still smiling. "I meant *bad* cop, not fat... Ah, hell. Poor Bim, he *tries* to lose weight, but it's his lifestyle, you know? He just can't do it. Still eats and lives like he's back in college, even though he dropped out after less than two years and never finished. And then, when he gets involved in these cases, he just eats more and more, trying to keep up his energy and stay focused. It's a vicious cycle."

Shelby nodded, filing away all the relevant information, but still feeling like there was something else about Bim that nobody was telling her. She'd figure it out later, after they cracked this Delia case.

"And from what he told me this morning, they've been doing things this way for twenty years now." Shelby sighed. "I'm just not sure why they hired me if they're not going to take me with them or let me actually interact with people."

"Look," Marly said, serious again, "I was the one who actually wrote up your job description. And I process every case that comes through here, from start to finish." She pointed at the files on her desk, stacked neatly next to her laptop. Marly didn't mess around. "There's more work here than Hank could ever get to in the next year. He's running from court to various lawyer's offices to surveillance gigs. But he drops everything when someone goes missing. We need all the help we can get so we don't let a single customer slip away."

Shelby was going to ask for a few of the files on the desk when Marly's purse, which was sitting on the other cushioned chair next to her desk, gave off an electronic trill that sounded like a cuckoo.

Marly grabbed for her cuckooing purse, pulled out a blue smartphone, and touched the screen. She grinned and shook her head.

"Juan. Texting me to tell us to keep it down. He must've heard us laughing. The guy doesn't miss a thing."

She tapped out a quick response, sent it with another cuckoo sound, and set the phone on top of her neatly stacked folders, still grinning.

"He likes to text instead of yell across the way. Or actually roll over here and talk, face-to-face and all, like normal people do. It's sort of cute."

"*Very* cute," Shelby agreed. She caught herself thinking about Juan, his legs, and his chair. Then she *realized* she was thinking about that instead of talking to Marly. And Marly had been watching her the whole time, reading her thoughts as if she'd had a big thought bubble over her head.

"Kick that door closed a sec," Marly said.

"It's okay," Shelby began, standing up. "You don't—"

"Just close the door."

Shelby did as ordered with her face burning.

"It's okay," Marly said. She leaned back in her chair and pulled her long black hair into a ponytail. "Juan doesn't like to talk about it, because he says he can't live in the past. I don't blame him."

Shelby became aware of the fact that she was still standing, so she settled back into her chair. She was totally going to have to get cushions in her office.

"We've known Hank since college at App State here, so he knows the whole story, as does Bim. It's only fair that we get you up to speed. It happened in Afghanistan. A roadside bomb, and it killed three other guys in Juan's platoon. Tore apart their Humvee, which didn't have any damn armor underneath it. Stupid. Juan wasn't even supposed to be out there in that mess, 'cause he worked in communications at the Army headquarters in Kandahar, but they needed tech guys like him up in Kabul for a couple weeks for a construction project. They were just riding from one place to another. No enemies around, no gunfire. Just a stupid bomb buried under the road. Wrong place, wrong time."

"God," Shelby said, her mouth dry.

"It was a rough time, almost ten years ago now. I had a brand-new baby, and my mama had just moved up here from Mexico, luckily, so I had some help. But Juan was in the hospital for a long time. His legs... They tried to save them, but the shrapnel..."

Marly sniffed suddenly and shook her head.

"It was hard, but we got through it. And Juan's *tough*, physically and mentally. He wouldn't let his injuries slow him down. And nowadays he gets to try out the latest wheelchairs and prosthetics from this research company he knows. He wants to be able to walk again, but with what he does right now, his high-tech wheelchair does the job really well. For now."

"That thing is *fast*," Shelby said. She wanted to get up and give Marly a hug, to do or say something, but she didn't have any other words.

Marly's phone cuckooed again.

"Speak of the devil, and he shall text you," Marly said, reading the phone's screen. "Juan says he's got your tablet all set up for you, along with all your logins and temporary passwords."

"I get a *tablet*?" Just the other day she'd been looking at iPads and other top-of-the-line gadgets, but couldn't justify the cost to get a really good one. Her ancient desktop running Windows XP was going to have to do for another year or two.

"Wait'll you see this thing," Marly said with a laugh, getting up and heading for the door. "Follow me."

* * * * *

Juan's office was wall-to-wall, floor-to-ceiling technology. He didn't have a big desk in the middle of the room like the other three offices. Instead he had tables pushed up against the walls, filled with hardware. Ten flatscreen monitors attached to two desktops and at least three laptops. A pile of phones sat on one table, while a trio of tablets rested on another. Not a single piece of paper littered the office. The room was extra cold to cool the six towers of loudly humming servers that took up two of the walls, thanks to the half-open window looking out onto the back parking lot of the former hotel.

Shivering, Shelby peeked out the window and saw that fresh snow covered the line of rhododendrons at the edge of the uneven asphalt.

"Welcome to Thunderdome!" Juan said. "Two men enter, one man leaves!"

"Omigod, I'm married to such a geek," Marly said, being careful not to step inside Juan's office nonetheless.

"Hey," Juan said to Marly. "When else do I get to show someone new around my server farm?"

The buzz of the servers forced Juan to almost yell as he spoke, but the sound didn't seem to bother him. It was about to make Shelby crazy. But Juan was in his element, rolling from one computer screen to the next, balancing his trusty blue laptop on his shortened right thigh with ease. Shelby wondered if he'd somehow velcroed or duct-taped the laptop to himself.

"Here ya go, new PI lady." Juan handed Shelby a sleek, bright-blue tablet that felt barely thicker than a couple sheets of paper.

"Thanks, Master Blaster," Shelby said, cradling the delicate-looking tablet in both hands. "I'll try not to break it."

Juan shot past Shelby, rolling suddenly backwards. She tried not to flinch, unsuccessfully, and gave him an exasperated smile instead. He'd come within two inches of rolling over the toes of her left foot.

"What brand is this?" she asked him, holding up the blue tablet. It wasn't an Apple product, but a brand she'd never heard of before called Tecknight, with a tiny knight on horseback etched into the case. All of the gadgets and computers in the room had the same kind of blue cases. "Is this some sort of black market brand?"

Juan just laughed.

"Can we step out into the lobby?" Shelby said at last, in a voice that was close to shouting. "This buzzing is about to make my head explode."

Juan beat her to the door. "Two men enter, one man leaves..." he called over his shoulder, then he was gone.

"He's usually not this bad," Marly apologized as Shelby walked out of Thunderdome with most of her hearing intact. "He'd just excited about this new case."

"Hey, I like Mad Max as much as the next gal," Shelby said. Juan heard her and rolled over to give her an enthusiastic fist bump. She'd thought he'd been a good fifteen feet away, under the dusty chandelier. The guy could *move* in that chair.

"You got your password for the tablet, right?" he asked her when they were safely away from the roaring servers. "I can write it down for you... if you want," he added, clearly not wanting to write anything down.

"Nope, I found it, along with all the other passwords on the tablet, in a file protected by a different password. Which I've also memorized."

"Can never be too safe," Juan said with a grin. "Not in our line of work. If someone steals your identity, you are hosed. And it's something that's easy to prevent."

"Thanks. I can't wait to start using this."

"Oh, I almost forgot." Juan reached into a side pocket on his chair, dug around for a moment with a pensive look on his face, and then pulled out a tiny blue keyboard. "This attaches to your tablet with magnets. You'll definitely need that with all the typing you're gonna be doing. It also doubles as a protective cover."

Shelby took the keyboard and tried to get it to fit onto the slim tablet. After a few tries, it snapped into place at an obtuse angle, and she had a perfect laptop-like setup.

"Sweet," she said. "Thank you!"

Juan gave her a wink and rolled back into his office without a sound. Shelby turned to Marly, who was staring at the open door to Juan's office with a bemused look on her face.

"I guess I'd better get some work done," Shelby said, feeling a surge of adrenaline at the thought. Finally. "I have to do some checking on nursing homes in the area."

"Sounds good," Marly said. "Enjoy!"

They went their separate ways back to their offices, leaving the big lobby empty once more.

* * * * *

Half an hour later, Shelby had learned that James Holhouser was a resident at Glenbridge Health and Therapy, and they were in the process of locking down the building looking for him when she called them. The nurse who answered the phone had a mountain drawl, and didn't want to trust Shelby's story about talking with James that morning, but when Shelby evoked Hank's name, the woman relaxed in an instant. Shelby reassured her that Hank would have James back by lunchtime, and the woman blessed Shelby's heart.

Grinning and shaking her head, Shelby texted Hank with the information about Glenbridge Health. She waited a moment for the text to go through, and then, just to be safe, sent the same text to Bim as well.

She put her long legs up on her desk, set the keyboard-tablet combo on her lap, and leaned back in her chair. Not bad. Though Tecknight really was a dumb brand name for such a slick, product.

Moving from the keyboard to the touchscreen and back to the keyboard, Shelby quickly filled a new document with everything she'd learned about James and his missing wife. A brain dump. It was something she'd done ever since starting out at the big insurance agency in Charlotte where she'd had her first PI job. Back when she had to document *everything*. And she never, ever left the office.

This job's gonna be different from that, she told herself as she typed out her report at near-Juan speeds. Even if I am still sitting in the

Finders, Inc. headquarters instead of getting out there. First days are always the hardest, on any job.

She read over the info she'd typed in, which barely filled one page, single-spaced. She still couldn't figure out why Delia might have taken off. They'd been married for most of their lives, and James seemed to truly love her. There were no odd looks when he spoke of her or answered questions about her. He didn't glance away or fiddle with his clothes or give any other hints that he wasn't being honest.

The only truly odd thing was the way he'd drifted off on them right in the middle of the conversation. He'd actually fallen *asleep* for a few seconds there. She hadn't had a chance to ask him—thank Hank for that, the controlling little dude—but Shelby had wanted to know if he had a touch of narcolepsy or early-onset dementia, and if so, was that why he was living in an assisted living facility like Glenbridge Health instead of at home with Delia? He seemed healthy otherwise. And how had Delia felt about that? Was she up to living on her own, after five decades of cohabitation?

More questions, more mysteries. Shelby loved this job.

And don't forget, she thought, typing more thoughts and theories into her document, which was now two pages, when James woke from his sudden little nap, he'd been surly. Snapping at Hank and...

"What was it he said?" she whispered to her empty office. She looked over at the metal folding chair where James had sat. Stared at it, as if it could talk. She put her legs back on the floor and rested her tablet on her desk, thinking and remembering.

Right after he'd woken up, James had been especially grumpy towards Hank. He'd forgotten who Hank was for a minute, and—*that* was it. He'd mistaken Hank for someone else.

"*Reminds of this thug fellow I met the other day*," Shelby said, speaking James' words as she typed them into her report.

They might need to keep an eye out for someone who looked like Hank. She knew that Boone and the surrounding mountain cities had a very small population of black people, which worked in their favor. It could be that this so-called thug fellow was involved somehow with Delia's absence. It wasn't the best lead ever, but it was a start.

Shelby had let her cup of coffee grow cold. She set it off to the far side of her otherwise empty desk and tapped the screen to pull up an Internet browser. Her brain felt a bit empty from all the typing she'd done—three pages now!—and she often found that surfing the various online news sites helped her back-brain make connections that her front-brain couldn't.

She fought the urge to check out CNN and Fox News and instead pulled up a couple mountain news sites for the local angle. There wasn't a big network affiliate up here—the closest was Charlotte, but that was a couple hours away—so she found the next best thing. She clicked through the *Mountain Times* website, scrolling past breaking news about road construction and the high school basketball team.

At the bottom of the page, in a flashing red box, Shelby found the next piece in the puzzle.

Silver Alert.

Apparently a man named Blake Barham had slipped away from a different nursing home than James' home. Those places needed to check their locks and upgrade their security, Shelby thought. Blake was seventy-seven, had minor dementia, and hadn't been seen at the home since 9 p.m. last night. The square image next to the article showed a smiling, balding man with white puffs of hair above either ear, like cotton balls.

Second one in three days. This was no coincidence.

Shelby read into the next paragraph, and stopped at the words "Mister Barham, a former professor at Appalachian State University..."

"No way," Shelby said. She was standing up now. She re-read the short article, which had been almost buried at the bottom of the page. As if nobody wanted to think about old people going missing.

That was two leads now, and counting, she thought, twisting off her keyboard and snapping it flat over the screen of her tablet. Can't wait to tell Bim and Hank—

She looked up when she heard the tap of boots out in the lobby. Tablet in hand, she got up and went to her office door to look out. Standing under the chandelier and tapping away at his phone was a tall, thin man with shaggy, prematurely gray-white hair who looked to be only a few years older than her. He wore a dark blue sport coat with jeans and cowboy boots.

Detective, Shelby thought right away. The fashion sense gives them away every time.

She wanted to get across the lobby to tell Marly about the second missing person, but the detective was right in her way. Marly's door was closed, as was Juan's, so neither of them had heard the guy walk in. She felt a flash of annoyance, but then she thought about how stupid she was being. This guy could have more info.

She cleared her throat and reminded herself that she worked here. That she *belonged.*

The detective looked up at her with sharp blue eyes. He had a moment of confusion as he tried to place her, unsuccessfully. Then he strode toward her, slipping the phone into his jeans pocket and holding out a hand to shake with a smile on his face.

"Hello there," he said. "I'm detective Charles Mathis with the Boone police department."

"Shelby Jamiston," she said, shaking hands with her best firm grip. "I'm the new investigator here. It's my second day."

Charles grinned even wider at that.

"Nice to meet you! Hank does good work here. Good, good work. I know you'll like it. Another investigator. Very interesting."

He pulled a card from inside his sports coat and slid it into her hand like a magician.

"We should do lunch sometime," he said, his blue eyes crinkling up as he gave her a smile. "Talk shop and all that."

Shelby was watching Charles, trying to figure him out, when she heard Marly's door open. Juan came rolling out of his office a heartbeat later. They both came hurrying up to her, as if needing to protect Shelby from the detective man.

"Chuck!" Juan called out, beating Marly to the chandelier by a good two seconds. "Long time no see, man!"

"Hey Charles," Marly said, less enthusiastically.

"Marly, Juan," Charles said. "I see you've got a new employee. Always good to see a local business grow and prosper."

Shelby felt the edges of Charles' card crinkle in her hand. Did he really just ask me out to lunch? That's two date offers in one day.

The four of them stood there in the middle of the lobby, waiting for someone to start talking. Shelby certainly wasn't going to be the one to break the silence, not knowing what the history was with the Finders and the local cops.

"So. I've got some questions for your boss," Charles said, finally. He gave them all an apologetic look that didn't really touch his eyes. "When will Hank be back?"

"Who knows?" Marly said.

But it was too late. Juan had his phone out, tapping the screen three times.

"They're about five minutes away," he said. "And heading here fast." He grinned at Shelby. "I love that tracking app."

"You can tell *us*, if you're in a hurry," Marly said. "We can pass it on. We're smart like that."

"Nah," Charles said. "I can wait. Sorry, it's confidential."

Shelby held on tight to her two new leads and watched the standoff in the lobby with a tiny, satisfied grin on her face. Who needed meditation, she thought, with a job like this?

Chapter Six

A kid in a candy store.

That's what she kept thinking about, every time she stepped into this small, bright white room filled with beakers, bowls, clear and yellow fluids, and bags and bottles of ingredients. The room was well-lit, the walls almost glowing white, but the labels on all the equipment and bags were blurry, *as if she'd kept her glasses off and couldn't see them clearly.*

Or maybe she was refusing to look too closely.

She walked over the creaking, bare-wood floor to the only window in the room, which had a thick red and blue beach towel hung over it like a curtain. She lifted it. Bright sunlight flooded the room and nearly blinded her at first. Blinking fast to clear her vision, she let the makeshift window blind drop back into place without ever getting a good look outside.

It didn't matter where she was. All that mattered was the work—the glorious work!—she had waiting for her here. She breathed in the pungent, nearly eye-watering odors filling the room and smiled. Today she'd start the latest recipe. They were going to do so much good here. It was just the kind of job she needed.

Forget feeling like a kid in a candy *store. This was like being a kid with a new* chemistry *set. Which was much better than candy...*

Bim opened his eyes and felt himself return like dead weight back to his own body in the passenger seat of Hanky J's car. As he reminded himself once again that he wasn't going to die, he watched the stubborn snow collect slowly on the windshield.

It's almost *April*, for crap's sake, he thought, waiting for his heartbeat to slow back down to normal. And this winter refuses to give up. Stupid winter.

While Hanky J and James finished up inside the house, Bim looked down at the three items Hank had given him from the Holhouser residence. A pen with a chewed-on cap (for some reason, chewed pens were great for picking up memories and making connections—probably due to the saliva, he figured) and two black earrings made of thin metal cut into delicate, abstract shapes. One earring was slightly bigger than the other. They reminded him of metal leaves falling from someone's ears instead of from a tree.

The connection he'd just made with Delia had felt like one of the weakest connections he'd ever experienced. At first he thought it was just fatigue from connecting so strongly with April Mae yesterday. Just his brain being a bit lazy, a bit overworked. Making him perform like a newbie.

But it was the fuzzy labels in his vision that did it for him. The woman whose mind he'd touched was deep in *denial* about something, to the point where she refused to might not really even be acknowledging what she was doing in that white room. Maybe it was a bit of dementia, or just delusions brought on by stress that kept her from really seeing what was right in front of her.

Also, Bim had kept waiting to get a sense of panic from her, or a whiff of fear. He'd felt plenty of both of those emotions from all the other connections he'd made in the past. Neither of those feelings came through in his initial mind-meld with her.

Guess I don't have enough information to go on, he thought.

Just her name, her former job, her husband's situation. Their house. Usually that was enough. But right now, other than the chemistry-set stuff in that white room, he had jack on where she might be.

His stomach let out a long rumble, one that Bim could actually see moving across his oversized beach ball of a gut. He'd only had a tiny bowl of oatmeal this morning instead of his usual fried drive-through triple breakfast from the closest fast-food joint.

This new diet was going to be torture for a few weeks, he figured. Then he'd start losing the weight and he'd get used to feeling hungry all the time. He hoped. He swallowed hard and forced himself to think of something other than lunch. It was only 11 a.m., anyway.

At last, James and then Hanky J stepped out of the Holhouser's front door and into the snow. His partner moved with that taut precision of his that told Bim he was irritated. They must not have found any evidence at all to show that Delia had been taken away. Looked like she'd just packed up her stuff for a trip somewhere, and she'd either neglected to tell James about it, or she'd told him and he'd forgotten. Bim was betting on the latter.

He watched his agitated partner wait for the old guy to catch up on their way down the snowy driveway. James looked even more worn-out and stooped than he had before they'd entered his house.

"Delia's *gone*," Bim murmured with a hint of a hard smile. He'd wanted to rile the old man up, just a bit, with his attempt at singing earlier. Just to gauge James' reaction.

If he'd actually offed his old lady—you never knew, these days—he'd have acted differently, more guilty or more edgy. But James had given Bim the reaction he'd been expecting. Just good old-fashioned anger tinged with fear of the unknown.

Hanky J did not approve of Bim's methods, but Bim didn't like to waste time if someone wasn't actually needing to be found. Time was of the essence when someone was truly missing. Hanky J knew that, but sometimes he wasn't willing to take that extra step like Bim was.

His belly gave a louder rumble this time, and Bim rubbed it absentmindedly, like an expectant mother late in her third trimester. For some reason, he kept thinking about the new PI, Shelby, whenever he had the urge to find a convenience store for some snacks. She was way less obvious than mean little April Mae had been yesterday when she first took a look at Bim, but Shelby still had that guarded look in her eyes that made Bim feel like she was trying to decide if she should feel sorry for him, or disgusted by him.

I have a way with the ladies like that, he thought. Like asking her to go get a friggin' latte with me. That was some kind of smooth, man.

Hanky J pulled open the back door for James. A cold blast of late-winter wind filled with pellets of snow blasted into the car along with him.

Back in the driver's seat, Hanky J gave Bim a look over the tops of his glasses: *Did you make a connection?*

Bim put Shelby out of his mind, reluctantly, and gave his boss a quick nod: *Yep. Connection made.*

"Good," Hanky J murmured. He turned to their client and passenger behind them. "We've got to get you home now, James."

Heavy sigh from the back seat.

"I figured as much," James said when the sigh was over.

"You're at Glenbridge Health, right?" Hanky J asked, peeking at his phone. Bim caught sight of a text on his rectangular screen. "Off Deerfield and Bamboo?"

"Um," James said after a long pause. "I... I *believe* so."

Eyebrows raised at that uncertain reaction, Bim waited for Hanky J to look his way. James was fading on them. And Bim had been expecting more questions from Hanky J about his connection with Delia, but then he assumed that Hanky J wanted to wait until James was off their hands. They began rolling downhill towards town.

Thinking about Shelby and their too-short conversation this morning got Bim thinking about another conversation he'd had earlier today, back when he was busy pacing the lobby. That one had gone on much too long.

It was Mom with her weekly update about Dad. She'd been staying with her sister, Aunt Betty, down the mountain in Lenoir, a half hour south of Boone. Bim didn't ask about the reasons for *that* setup, because that was how Mom and Dad rolled. They'd fight like crazy about some stupid thing when they were together, then make up and be good for a week or two. Then things would heat up again, and Mom would get tired of it and need a break.

Mostly they fought about Dad and his bad luck with jobs and money. He liked to gamble, but he liked drinking even more. Bim was amazed he'd survived his own childhood at all, though he did have fond memories of getting away during most summers and spending them with his grandparents in their little cabin outside the town of

Banner Elk. Getting away from the yelling and the drinking and the irregular meals had been like Christmas every day for young Bim.

"He's feeling poorly," Mom had told Bim this morning, each word dripping with drama. "He really would like you to stop by, spend some time. He's been out of work since after Christmas, and it's just him up there on our mountain."

Just thinking about her words now made Bim want to get up and start pacing around. But he was wedged here in the front seat of the car, and Hanky J was trying to find the turn to James' nursing home east of town. Bim told him to back up and turn right at the street he'd blown past a minute earlier. In Hanky J's defense, the street sign had been half-covered with snow.

"Has he been to see a doctor?" Bim had asked Mom, ignoring her guilt trip about visiting Dad.

"Of course not. Stubborn old mule. Maybe he'd go if *you* asked him. Go up and see him, Bim."

"What was the fight about this time?"

"We're not fighting," Mom said, all innocent and *How could you even think that?*

"I'll see what I can do," Bim said after a long, guilt-ridden silence on the phone.

That was right about the time that Shelby Jamiston had walked through the front entrance to Finders, Inc., and she'd taken his breath away. That light brown hair with hints of red to it, those long legs, those ridiculously stylish heels. Pale white skin that Bim might have compared to porcelain if nobody else was around. He could make out her curves even with her heavy winter coat on, which told him she was no skinny girl but a real woman with some bark to her bite.

And of course, his immediate reaction to her unexpected appearance was to turn his back on her as fast as he could.

Ladykiller, he thought. That's me.

"There's the entrance," he said now to Hanky J, pointing through a wall of fat snowflakes coming at them.

"Oh my," James said from the back seat. "They are not going to be happy with *me*."

"I'll walk you in," Hanky J said, and then he turned to Bim and spoke in a quiet voice. "We'll be back in a few. See what you can do about... you know."

"Yeah, boss. Will do."

With the engine idling and blowing warm-ish air onto Bim, he watched Hanky J and James make their way carefully over the fresh snow on the ground and past the square columns of the big, overhanging front entrance.

Bim tried not to get too emotionally involved with the clients, but watching poor James creep back to his new home in the cold, wearing his best suit jacket over his pajama shirt, filled him with determination to get a better sense of where the hell Delia Holhouser might be. She was probably with a friend—*not* a boyfriend—for a few days, probably someone out of town. It didn't feel like an abduction, and really, who would want to abduct an older person anyway? Bim didn't think that angle worked at all, so he dropped it.

Instead, he closed his eyes and wrapped his thick hand around the mismatched earrings and the chewed-up pen.

And he waited.

The wind whipped against the side of the car, rocking it as if a couple big, drunk, college guys were out there pushing on it, trying to tip it over.

Bim exhaled and waited some more.

And waited.

Shivering now, feeling a tickle of panic invade his bloodstream and quicken his pulse, Bim closed his eyes tighter.

Squeezed the earrings and pen harder.

Thought about that white room full of chemicals and equipment.

Was it like the Chem lab back at Watauga High? he wondered, waiting for the connection. Or maybe someplace at the university?

Bim opened his eyes and let Delia's belongings drop from his numb hand.

This has never happened before, he thought at first, reaching down around his belly and big legs and feet to try and retrieve the dropped items. He couldn't reach them around his own bulk.

And then his heart sunk, because he *did* remember this happening before.

"Four times," he whispered.

If he had any room at all to move inside Hanky J's shitty little Ford Escort, he would've pulled his wallet out of his back pocket to look at the names of those four people again. The four they'd *lost*, permanently. He definitely didn't want to add Delia Holhouser to the list. The other four had died before he and Hanky J could find and save them. The connection had ended at the same time that their lives did. Like throwing a switch. Or pulling a trigger.

Bim reached down once more for Delia's earrings and pen, making the shocks of the Escort squawk and squeak from the effort. But he couldn't do it. His head started to spin just from the effort.

And that led to an avalanche of pity that Bim unleashed upon himself.

Fat and worthless. No way you're gonna lose weight. No way would a woman like Shelby Jamiston have any interest in you. No way you have any kind of special powers. No way. No way. No *way*!

He was buried under his own deluge of angst when Hanky J touched his shoulder. Bim nearly screamed out in shock and awe.

"Bim!" Hanky J shouted. He'd brought a wave of cold air and wet snow into the car with him, a wave that Bim hadn't felt until just then. "Snap out of it, man!"

Bim sat up straight and had to forcibly remove his clawed hands from his face. He didn't remember putting them there, much less squeezing so hard he could feel ten throbbing circles all around his cheeks and forehead.

"I'm *losing* it," he whispered. His vision blurred as sudden tears filled his eyes with his confession. "I could barely connect with her earlier. And now she's gone. She's *gone*, man!"

"Here," Hanky J said, slipping a tiny hand around the twin tree trunks of Bim's shins. He snagged the earrings and pen from the floor with ease, and he now held them two inches from Bim's face.

"You ain't lost *anything*, bud."

Bim refused to touch the items.

"I can't do it. There's nothing there."

Ever since he'd discovered that he could touch someone else's mind and read their thoughts—just for a second or two at first, when he was in his late teens—he'd been afraid that it was all a fluke. That it would just go away, and he'd have nothing all over again. He'd just be the fat kid who grew into a fat teen, and then became a fat, sad grown-up.

"I'll hang onto them, for now," Hanky J said after a long pause. "Just let me know when you want 'em back, okay?"

Bim couldn't even look at Hanky J. He heard him slip the earrings and pen into a pocket on his coat.

"Go ahead and fire me," Bim mumbled.

"*What*?"

Bim looked up at that. He hadn't heard that kind of heat in Hanky J's voice in a long time—at least not directed at him.

"Just get rid of me," Bim said, glancing at Hanky J and almost recoiling at the simmering anger behind Hanky J's chunky black glasses. "If I can't connect to people for you, what good am I?"

Hanky J slapped the steering wheel with his left hand and put the car into reverse with his right.

"No way I'm even going to answer that question for you, Bim Mayer." He let out a quick laugh. "*Just get rid of me*," he said in a dopey voice that, not surprisingly, had some similarity to Bim's voice from a moment ago. "*Just fire me and put me out of my misery*."

"Knock it off," Bim said, hands clenching into fists. "I was serious—"

"*Just fire me, boss—*"

"Stop it!

"*What good am I—*"

"Stop!"

Bim was in the process of reaching over to grab Hanky J by the lapels when something exploded against his leg. He yelled and slapped a hand on it as another explosion hit it.

Then he realized he'd set his phone to vibrate mode.

"Excuse me for one second," he muttered to Hanky J, embarrassed. He worked hard to extricate his phone from the pocket of his sweat pants, with Hanky J's mocking voice echoing in his ears. In the meantime, Hanky J turned the car around again in the snowy lot of the nursing home, and he was driving them back toward town and their headquarters.

Bim noticed that the phone number was a new one to him before he tapped an icon to take the call.

"Hey Bim, where are you?" a familiar female voice asked as soon as he put the phone to his ear. Marly, talking fast.

Behind the wheel, Hanky J silently asked who was on the phone. Bim held up a hand for him to hold his horses.

That's what you get, he thought, for mocking me in my moment of need, boss-man.

"Heading back now," Bim said into the phone, "minus one escaped nursing home resident. What's going on there?"

"Tell Hanky to hurry up. We got stuff happening here. Shelby's got some news, and Charles is here wanting to talk to you both. Okay, here's Shelby."

Bim had opened his mouth four times to try and say something to Marly, but she was too fast for him each time. And now there was just silence. Bim pictured Marly handing the phone to Shelby—the 704 area code he'd seen right before answering meant this was most likely the new lady's cell.

"Hey Bim, this is Shelby."

Now that he had the opportunity to speak, Bim found himself unable to do so. His tongue had somehow glued itself to the roof of his mouth. He thought of Shelby's crooked smile and her blue eyes, and it became hopeless.

"So listen," Shelby said, unnecessarily, "we've been doing some digging here at the office—you should see Juan going to town with his Google searches and database hacks—and making some calls. Soon as you two get back here we'll go over all we've learned. But yeah, like Marly said, there's a detective here. Skinny guy, almost white hair, but he can't be much older than us. Do you *trust* this guy, Bim?"

Bim's tongue finally got unstuck. With a glance at Hanky J, who was looking tired and almost as hungry as Bim felt right now, he nodded at the phone. Then he cleared his throat and found his voice again.

"Yeah, definitely. Charles is a good detective. Just don't volunteer any information to him, and you'll be fine."

"*Charles* is there?" Hanky J blurted out. "What happened?"

"Chill, man," Bim said to Hanky J.

Into the phone, he said, "So what happened?"

Shelby gave a frustrated snort. "Says he needs to talk to Hank right now. Like he'll talk to us later, if he so chooses. Whatever."

"Yeah," Bim said with a laugh. "That sounds like Charles. He's a little paranoid about stuff. If you knew who he worked with, you'd understand."

Bim could tell that Hanky J was driving faster now, even with the snow falling harder. He gripped the phone tightly with his left hand and held onto the handle above the door with his right.

"Yeah," Shelby said back to him, a glimmer of pride in her voice now. "But that's not all. Charles can keep his secrets. I found something *very* interesting online this morning."

Bim closed his eyes, not wanting to get sucked into this case any longer. Not when it was going to give him so much grief trying to connect to Delia.

"Okay," he said, then he had to squeeze his eyes shut again as Hanky J ran a red light to get onto 321 heading south. "What did you find out?"

"There's been *another* one," Shelby said in a cool voice. "Another older person has gone missing. Second one in three days. Well, second one that we *know* about, that is. A man in his late seventies this time. And no, it wasn't James sneaking off from his nursing home, either. And get this—he also used to teach at the university. See ya soon," she said, and then killed the call.

Bim realized his mouth was hanging open. He closed it and put away his phone so he could swipe at Hanky J's coat pocket until his partner handed him back the earrings and the chewed-on pen.

"We got us a *case*," he told Hanky J with a grin.

Chapter Seven

"Gimme a minute," Hank said to Bim when they arrived at their headquarters.

He left the car running, the engine rattling off an uneven, slightly unhealthy beat. He wasn't surprised to see that Bim hadn't made a move to open his door either. Despite his enthusiasm about the case a minute ago, Hank knew the big guy was in no rush to go inside and have to deal with Charles. Their mutual dislike had to do with some ancient history related to Bim's father, who had been getting into trouble for all of Bim's life. As soon as they were inside and dealing with Charles, Bim would no doubt find a way to get out of there as fast as he could.

We all have our weaknesses, Hank thought, remembering his brief stop at Glenbridge Health. He'd had to use all of his willpower to not run screaming from the place after dropping off James. It was a clean and relatively modern facility, as far as places like that went. But the home had an air of desperation and defeat that hung over it like a cloud.

As a self-starter all of his life, Hank couldn't think of a worse place to wait for his life to end. He could understand why James would want to sneak away, and why he'd looked so dejected at having to return.

The suspicious looks that the nurse manning the reception desk had given him on his way in and on his way out hadn't helped his attitude much, either.

Hank was also irritated—and he didn't want to admit it, but he was also a little bit hurt—that Marly had called Bim instead of him. He knew if he tried to pump Bim for information right now, Bim would just zip his lip and laugh at Hank. All Bim had told him from his brief call from the other Finders was that another old person had gone missing.

I should fire them all, he thought.

The ludicrous nature of that idea—which was just as over-the-top as the way he'd goaded Bim a few minutes earlier about him asking to be fired—made him laugh. From his hangout in the passenger seat, Bim gave Hank a raised eyebrow, but said nothing as he drummed his thick fingers on his wide left leg.

Now, Hank thought, still smiling, I think I can deal with Charles Mathis from the Boone P.D.

"Who knows," he said in the overly warm car, mostly to himself. "Maybe Charles will have something useful for us this time. Instead of harassing us about jurisdiction and following his rules. Maybe he'll actually have some insight into this case, and our *two* missing persons."

Bim unbuckled his seatbelt at last and paused.

"Charles? *Insight*? I doubt that."

Hank shut off the car and opened his car door at last, welcoming the cold wind in his face and in his sore and tired eyes. His experiment with getting four hours of sleep per night was starting to wear thin, though he'd only been doing it for two and a half weeks. After three weeks, it would become habit, he knew—part of his daily routine. At which point he'd be the most productive person anyone could ever know.

Outside, the snow was letting up, but they must have gotten a good three to four inches already, and it was just now noon. Hank hoped that Delia—and the Silver Alert guy that Bim had told him about—weren't out there somewhere in it, lost and confused. Slowly freezing to death.

After he kicked snow and slush off his boots outside the front door, Hank entered the lobby. He immediately noticed that the smell of mildew inside the office was mostly gone, and the scent of fresh paint had also mostly dissipated, leaving just the odors of dust and coffee to compete with one another in his nose. It was a definite improvement over the stench of dry rot in here just a month ago when he'd bought the place.

And there, standing under the chandelier, was detective Charles Mathis, wearing his usual serious expression along with a dark blue sport coat, jeans, and cowboy boots. He was chatting with Juan, arms crossed, looking extremely impatient, while Hank could hear Shelby and Marly talking softly in Marly's office.

As predicted, Bim took a quick detour away from the chandelier and headed toward the coffee pot, muttering something about not wanting to deal with any dicks right now.

Tread lightly, Hank reminded himself. Charles was a good detective, but he considered *everyone* a suspect, and he also considered Finders, Inc. the competition when the cases got tough.

"Charles!" Hank called out, trying to muster up some enthusiasm for the visit. "Glad you were able to find us! What do you think of the new place?"

A quick smile flitted over the detective's gaunt face. "It's got character," he said, and then added, "just like the people using it."

"I'm gonna take that as a compliment," Hank said. He hoped his big, aw-shucks smile didn't look too fake. "Did you give him the nickel tour, Juan?"

"Nah," Charles said before Juan could answer. Juan shot him a dirty look and rolled back to his office, clearly relieved to be off babysitting duty. "I don't have time for that. They said you'd be back any minute—*they* being Marly and your new hire, thanks for telling me about that, by the way—so I wanted to be here as soon as you got back. How's Bim the Mayer doing? I saw him duck out of here as soon as he saw me."

"Bim is Bim," Hank said. "He helped us find April Mae yesterday, along with the rest of the team. The Observer had a great write-up about that case. You might have seen that."

In the time it would've taken a normal person to respond with "Nice work" or "Congrats," Charles just nodded and stared down at Hank.

"So," Hank said, unfazed by Charles and his lack of social graces, "what brings you by?"

Charles' face tightened up a few degrees more.

"Can we talk privately, Johnson?"

Hank nodded at his corner office, and Charles was off, his long strides eating up the lobby floor.

Show-off, Hank thought, fifteen feet behind him.

When Hank dropped into his chair in his office with the door securely closed behind them, Charles dropped a one-word bomb:

"Meth."

"No way," Hank said, leaning forward with a loud squeak from his chair. "I thought that trend was all over with up here, especially with the college kids."

"I wish," Charles said, crossing his leg over his knee so he could tap the heel of his cowboy boot absently with his forefinger and thumb. "Looks like there's a new supplier in town, and someone's been getting the word out. Probably dropping free samples at frat parties. These kids should *know* better. And it's not just the college kids. We've run across a couple locals in possession of the junk, too. All in the past two to three weeks."

Hank fought the urge to get up and pace.

He *hated* drugs, hated everything about them—how they altered a person's mental and physical state, how they made a person check out of reality, how they hooked the user and took over the user's life. His younger brother William had tried pretty much every kind of drug back in his late teens and early twenties, and by the time William was twenty-five, he'd lost pretty much all interest in being a productive part of society. Hank hadn't spoken with him in six years, and didn't know—didn't *want* to know—where William had ended up after drifting out of Boone all those years ago. All thanks to drugs.

"Who'd be stupid enough to start making meth around here?" he asked Charles. "You guys cleared out all the meth labs what, three years ago? No way this is a local job."

"We picked up some of the meth and I've got our lab guys in Charlotte analyzing it. It's a new formula, I think. Pretty potent stuff, from the reports I've seen—we've had three college kids show up in the ER in the past couple of days already, close to overdosing on the stuff. It's also really, really flammable. Not just the ingredients when they're putting the junk together, but the finished product. Can't even smoke it, so you gotta snort it."

Hank rubbed his face and felt a sympathetic series of twinges inside his nasal cavity all the way up to his brain. *Nasty.*

Charles watched him closely. After a long, awkward moment, he nodded to himself, straightened up, and put both booted feet onto the floor with a clomping sound.

"So this is the first you've heard of all this," he said.

Hank sighed and nodded, feeling like he'd let down the detective, along with all the citizens of Boone and the surrounding towns.

"It's been a crazy-busy week with half a dozen different cases hitting at the same time, and then we were out all day yesterday," he said. He stopped when it sounded like he was making excuses. "But yeah, we've seen nothing about meth in any of our cases. Though we do have a bit of a backlog..."

Hank smacked the top of his desk and popped to his feet, unable to sit still any longer. There was something about today's case that he wanted to double-check, along with the rest of the files that he knew Marly had sitting on her desk.

"Say, you wanna come to a quick staff meeting?" he asked Charles. "We love having guests."

Charles looked like he'd rather have a molar removed without anesthesia. He stood up as well.

"Nah. I gotta go run down some leads on these college kids who nearly OD'd. But you keep me in the loop on this one, Johnson. If you come across anything, call me."

"Same goes for you. You know we're good for it."

Charles nodded once, quickly, and stepped closer to Hank, so close Hank could smell his aftershave and his coffee breath.

"We gotta nip this shit in the *bud* before we have an outbreak on our hands, you get me? You may want to check to see if the, ah, *usual suspects* have been up to anything nefarious. Just saying. Might be better if *you* talk to them before me. Or the state inspectors, if and when they come to town."

Hank met his gaze, forcing down his rising emotions. He didn't like the insinuations Charles was making, but based on the team's blood relations—like his brother William and Bim's father Ozzy, for starters—Charles probably had a pretty good case to be suspicious. That was probably the real reason Charles had dropped by today. Digging for connections.

"We'll take that under consideration," Hank said at last. "Sure you don't want to stay for the meeting? We'll brew up some fresh coffee and everything."

"Nah," Charles said again, his serious expression breaking up into an actual smile. He stepped toward the door. "As *fun* as it sounds to sit in yet another long-ass meeting, I've really got to run. Call or text me when you get something, okay?"

"Of course."

Hank followed him back out into the lobby, breathing a silent sigh of relief that the big, musty room was deserted, with everyone in their respective offices, working away. He saw Charles shoot a long look at Shelby's half-open office door, as if pondering stopping by and chatting. Then he picked up the pace and left, with a no-look wave in Hank's direction.

"Crap," Hank said, staring up at the chandelier with its finger-sized rectangles of dusty glass that reminded him all too much of shards of crystal meth. He hated that people snorted or injected or smoked or drank all those chemicals to lift them up or to slow them down, or to take away their pain. Hank only took aspirin if he felt like he was knocking at death's door. He preferred a supremely healthy lifestyle over chemicals.

Speaking of which, he knew he needed to carve out some time for a quick workout. No wonder he was feeling anxious and edgy, But first he had to get everyone together and address the new meth problem.

Hank started for Marly's office, and then he pulled up short.

Chemicals, he thought. *Chemistry.*

"Holy crap," he said, charging towards Marly's office at a full run.

She jumped at his sudden, breathless appearance at her door. With a guilty look on her face, she stopped talking into her phone and tapped her screen, and just as quickly closed the paper file she'd been looking at.

Probably part of our backlog that she hadn't yet shared with me, Hank thought, itching for the file and the information it contained.

"You okay, boss?"

"We need to call a meeting," he said. "Ten minutes, out here in the lobby. 11:55. I'll go get Bim. And bring all the files, including the Holhouser one. Tell Juan he can order pizzas from Hungry Howie's if he wants."

"Will do!" Marly said, already gathering the files, her laptop, and her phone.

Ignoring the sudden rumble of hunger in his belly—he'd sworn off lunches long ago—Hank went out into the cold and snow to the six-sided building next to the pool that Bim had commandeered for his own office.

His phone buzzed in his pocket as a gust of wind cooled the fresh sweat that had sprung up on his forehead. He checked his phone, and as usual it was a text from Mom, asking him how he was and—of course—if he'd talked to Miranda. With a grimace, Hank slid the phone back into his jeans pocket and rapped on the door to Bim's poolside office.

When nobody answered, he opened the door and found Bim covered in a ratty green blanket, sleeping precariously on the old couch that was pushed against two of the glass walls overlooking the frozen pool. Unpacked boxes sat stacked on the floor, and the far wall was covered in flattened cardboard that hid the strange, psychedelic mural painted onto it. The place was chilly even with the two space heaters running full-blast next to the couch.

Hank paused, not wanting to wake the big guy. He had a peaceful smile on his wide, furry face, as if he was dreaming of hula girls and hot sand. But then Hank remembered all the trouble Bim's dad Ozzy had caused over the years, and he slammed the door behind him.

Bim woke with a start, yelling something that sounded like "Better than candy!" before he sat up on the creaking couch.

"What the *hell*, man?" Bim said, rubbing his eyes and pushing the hair out of his face.

"This is it, my friend," Hank said. "It's time for our first staff meeting here at Finders, Inc. HQ."

* * * * *

The first staff meeting at Finders, Inc., HQ began at exactly eleven minutes past noon, sixteen minutes later than Hank had hoped.

Everyone had circled up in the arm chairs below the big chandelier, grabbing slices of pizza and cans of soda from the rickety table. Bim was the last to show up, of course, and Hank had been tempted to start without him and force him to catch up on his own.

But there had been something in Bim's eyes back in his six-sided office a half hour ago that had made Hank feel a bit more patient with him. He'd looked desperate, and possibly even scared, when Hank had woken him there. Hank figured Bim was still having troubles tuning into Delia's unique mindset. That hadn't happened often, but when it did, Hank knew it haunted the big guy.

"So good," Juan said after eating half a slice of Hungry Howie's specialty with pepperoni, ham, mushroom, and peppers in one bite. He'd made sure to take advantage of the situation when Hank had given him the green light to order in lunch.

Hank politely declined the pizza, and then everyone went silent as Bim also chose not to indulge himself.

"*What*?" Bim said from his chair, gazing wide-eyed at the pizza boxes quickly being emptied on the table in front of him. "Maybe I'm not hungry, okay?"

Finally, Hank couldn't wait any longer. He'd waited long enough since Charles had strutted out of the office.

"Okay, you all can listen while you eat," he began, popping up out of his chair. "Here's the situation. The Boone police are dealing with a meth outbreak."

As he shared everything Charles had told him, except for the part about checking on the so-called usual suspects, Hank watched how Shelby reacted to the information. He wondered what kind of experiences she'd had down in Charlotte, working with drug problems at the big insurance agency down there. Probably not many. They'd had relatively few here, luckily. She paid close attention to all he said, tapping notes one-handed onto her Tecknight tablet without even looking down at it.

Next to her, Marly's face had grown red as Hank talked about the issues with meth hitting town again. Her good friend Nina had gotten mixed up with meth right after 9/11, when the whole country seemed to be falling apart. Right at the same time Juan was called up to active duty from the National Guard to go to Afghanistan. Nina's husband Jack had also gotten the call, and while he was away, Nina had spent her days slowly going crazy, according to Marly. Which led to Nina mixing up with the wrong people, and she'd gotten hooked on meth.

"Marly," Hank said when he'd finished up his recitation of most of what Charles had told him. "What kind of professor did Delia Holhouser used to be?"

Marly sat up straight as if poked in the side. She peeked into the top file on her lap and found the information in a heartbeat. "Organic and Biological Chemistry."

Shelby stopped tap-typing for a moment next to her. "The other guy who just went missing, Blake Barham. What'd he teach?"

Juan was doing some fierce typing of his own.

"What the *hell*," he said, staring at the screen of his well-used laptop. "He was in Chemistry, too. Physical Chemistry, and some Physics. A few Astronomy classes also. Jack of all trades, back in the day."

Hank smacked his fist victoriously into his open palm, just as he became aware that he was pacing around the circle of chairs, like a runner doing laps. He forced himself to slow down and get under control, even as Juan confirmed his own hastily made theory.

"I think I used to watch this show on TV," Bim said, picking up a box of pizza from the chair next to him. He glanced around at the others to see if any of them—other than Hank—were watching him. They weren't. "Except that was about a *high school* teacher making meth, not retired college profs."

"Okay," Hank said, pointing at Bim. "I'm glad you played the 'Breaking Bad' card, because that's *exactly* what popped into my head, too."

"But you think someone's *kidnapping* retired Chemistry professors?" Shelby said. She'd set her tablet next to her in the chair so she could hold a slice of pizza. "Seems like a big risk, just to make some meth. Even if it's chemically perfect meth."

"No way," Bim said with a loud fake yawn as he tried to casually open the pizza box. "Too big a risk."

Hank's phone buzzed again, and he nearly slapped at it like it was an annoying fly.

"I'm open to any and all theories," he said. "We don't have a specific case dealing with meth right now—" he stopped and glanced over at Marly "—well, that is, as far as I know, we don't, right Marly?"

"Let me check," she said, digging into her folders. "I thought I saw something from last month."

At the same time, Juan began typing in his usual aggressive fashion. "I'll comb my databases for meth busts and any references to it in the local media in the past five years. One sec..."

Hank looked over at Bim, who was now scarfing *two* slices of pizza stacked on top of the other with his eyes closed tightly. He'd held out a good five minutes longer than Hank had thought he would.

In the chair next to Bim, Shelby stared up at the chandelier, lost in thought.

Hank smiled at the energy his team was generating here.

Sheer brainpower, he thought. Well, except for Bim over there, inhaling all the pizza that's left over.

"Good pie," Bim said with his mouth full, as if talking to himself. He swallowed with a guilty glance over at Shelby, but she was now busy tapping away on her tablet and distractedly chewing on her bottom lip.

"Okay," Juan began. "I got—"

"Here's something," Marly said at the same time. "This guy—"

Juan sighed and gave his wife a grin.

"You first," he said, and then his laptop beeped once, loudly.

At the same time, the alarm Juan had installed that morning began honking out its emergency alarm.

"What the hell?" Bim said, covering his ears with greasy fingers.

Hank was already sprinting to the control panel for the new alarm, and as he ran he could hear Juan swearing in Spanish behind him, loud enough to be heard over the alarm. That was never a good sign.

With his ears ringing, he punched in his password and explained to the operator on the other end of the communication system for the alarm that all was well. He felt a pang of dread as he said that, wondering if he was speaking the truth. The hotel grounds were big, and someone could've tried sneaking into one of the rooms again. He'd have to take a look, but not right now.

"That was weird," he said a moment later in the sudden, post-alarm silence. He turned back to the others, just in time to see Juan speed off into his server-filled office.

"What's going on?" he called to Marly on his way back to the circle of chairs under the chandelier. "I don't like it when he moves that fast."

Marly and the others were all standing now, looking at Juan's office.

"Me neither," she said. "He said something about us being hacked. But that's impossible, not with all the safeguards he's got in place. Impossible..."

Shelby held up her blue tablet and tapped it a few times.

"Really?" she said. "Look at this thing."

She held it up so Hank and the others could see the numbers, letters, and symbols spinning across her screen like something out of "The Matrix." Finally the tablet made an ominous popping sound and went dark.

"Now that's messed up," Bim said. "Not sure the warranty will cover that."

In his pocket, Hank's phone buzzed again, a long buzz that didn't seem like it would ever end, and then did a quick little buzz that had a strange sense of finality to it. He pulled it out and looked at it, and the dead black screen didn't surprise him.

"Yeah," Hank said, his voice tight with rage. "Juan's right. We just got *hacked*."

Chapter Eight

Juan was furious.

The morning had started out great, with the electrical guys finally getting the wiring done the way he wanted it, then this new missing-person case had popped up out of nowhere. The new hire seemed pretty cool, for a PI, and she'd totally gotten his Mad Max reference.

And then it had all turned to shit in the space of ten seconds. It wasn't just the hotel alarm—he never trusted those things, because they were way too sensitive and way, way too much of a pain in the butt to disable once they went off. Nor was it the way his laptop had given him the blue screen of death before going black altogether. Someone had gotten to half of the *servers*, too. Bypassed all his safeguards and firewalls and got control of them in a hostile takeover. All of their data was now at risk.

He rolled from one keyboard and screen combo to the next, wishing his office was bigger, the whole time sweating and also wishing his office was *colder*. At times like this, his military training kicked in, and the rest of the world fell away, but he could never keep himself from sweating like a pig. Even after the explosion in Afghanistan, he'd been slippery with hot sweat mixed with his own blood—

"Stop," he ordered himself. He'd been on the verge of hyperventilating, and his vision had gone blurry as he tried to make sense of what he was seeing on his screens.

The team needs you, he continued silently. Don't lose focus and go all PTSD right now. You're better than that, man.

He could sense some, if not all of the others right outside his office door, waiting for an update, but they knew better than to poke their heads in right now. Marly would make sure of that. She knew he needed a few minutes of complete privacy to get this fixed.

He went to his biggest and newest desktop computer, which sat closest to the half-open window, and logged in. He jumped right to the command line and started up a series of his own personalized scripts and batch files. His wrists gave a warning tingle of carpal-tunnel pain that he ignored as he typed faster.

Three of their servers were already dead in the water, he had to admit. But this computer and the other three servers were behind his best security, and they were still running. All the data on the dead servers was encrypted, but Juan didn't trust that someone with enough motivation and hacking power wouldn't get through that encryption eventually. He was so glad he didn't let Hank talk him into saving everything up to the cloud.

Thirty minutes passed, then sixty, then ninety. Juan barely noticed until he started to shiver. The sweat had dried on his forehead, and he'd revived the three dead servers and was scrubbing them clean with various antiviral scripts he'd created and borrowed from other code-monkeys like himself. He'd even fixed his trusty laptop.

And best of all, he had gathered some key bits of information about the person—or *persons*, more likely—who'd hacked them. At least one of them was up north, in the state of Delaware somewhere, and someone else was in Idaho. Or maybe that was where they were bouncing their location from, to keep him off-balance.

I don't *get* off-balance, Juan thought as he pushed his chair away from the row of computers. He reveled in the hum of all the servers running at full-speed again, and he double-checked the list he'd made on his laptop about the hackers.

This was gonna be fun, he thought. They'll regret screwing with the Chief Technical Officer of Finders, Inc.

Juan rolled out of his office, pumped to share his success with the others. But the lobby was empty, and all the office doors were closed. He could've sworn he heard the door to Shelby's office close just a second ago.

"All clear," he said to himself. "No need to *worry*, folks..."

As he spoke, he felt sudden fatigue drop on him like a leaded blanket. It was almost three o'clock in the afternoon, and he felt like he'd just woken from a dream. His lower back hurt, and his hands throbbed from repetitive stress. Too much typing and mousing mixed with the wheel work on his chair. He was supposed to wear gloves with his chair, but they always slowed him down while he was typing.

And he'd been up way too late the past few nights, playing old-school Atari video games with Bim the night before last, and then last night he'd been watching some old sci-fi movie on Netflix while trying to fix Marly's personal laptop that little Bonita had filled with viruses in the past few months. The Tech Support never ended, even at home.

He needed to work on his teammates' laptops and tablets, get them cleaned up and fully functional again, but the closed doors had killed his victorious mood.

They should've been waiting, he thought, and then thrown me a ticker-tape parade for what I just did back there.

"Fine," he said. "Their hardware can wait. I got plenty of meth research to do, and lots of Silver Alerts to track down. No worries."

Juan rolled back into his office, trying to decide how many years to go back with his research, when the hotel alarm began blaring again, and he heard his servers come to an unceremonious stop once again.

* * * * *

Marly hadn't wanted to leave the lobby—she felt like she was letting Juan down by not being right there for him—but after fifteen minutes of listening to his furious typing and heavy breathing and cursing, she couldn't just *stand* there. The others had already crept back to their offices to try to get their gadgets working again on their own. But she had to peek in on him before she bailed.

He was moving fast, and he looked to be in hog's heaven. He was so busy sliding from one machine to the next that he didn't even notice her.

She always worried about Juan in situations like this, when his stress levels got elevated. She knew he'd probably have trouble sleeping tonight after all this, the chaos reminding him of the war and the day of the bomb. She wanted to slip in and put a hand on his back, just to let him know he wasn't in a war zone anymore, but he wouldn't want that right now. He just needed time to focus.

Take it to 'em, Juan Carlos, she thought, aiming good vibes in his direction before she moved away from his chilly server cave.

Back in her own office, Marly kept her laptop closed. She didn't need it to pull together her thoughts about the paper files covered in sticky notes and spread out in front of her on her desk. Her smartphone was still up and running, thanks to all the security features and hacks than Juan had installed on it the moment they both got their matching versions. She picked it up and tapped on the voice memo app.

"Douglas Slocumb," she said into her phone, reading from a file and recording her words. "Forty-five years old—*damn*, that's about the same age as the rest of us, and look at how *he* ended up—with a history of drug abuse and two arrests for carrying around enough crystal meth that he got hit with intent to sell. And that's what he's doing time for now at Mountain View Correctional Institution. This was the third strike for him, got the max of five years. But here's the catch: his common-law wife came in back on February twentieth and said he was set up. She wanted us to investigate, but it looks like..." Marly picked up the file and squinted at the hand-written sticky note that Hank had left at the bottom of the file. "...Ah, okay. Hank said we don't have time right now to investigate, in his words, 'repeat drug offenders.' That it was a quote-unquote rabbit hole. Innnteresting."

Marly paused her phone and read through the rest of the file. The Slocumb name sounded familiar, and she knew who to ask about him. Bim knew everyone up here in the area, as well as who was related to whom, and what their family history was, especially if there was bad blood. But Marly also knew Bim, and she'd need to do something for him to sweeten the deal. Even if it was just bringing him a cup of coffee or a slice of pizza. For Bim, he never scratched your back if you didn't get out the back-scratcher first and go to town.

Marly shuddered a bit at that mental image. At first she'd been disgusted by Bim's size, and how he seemed to have no regard for what other people thought of him. And his penchant for speaking his mind, no matter how rude, used to really annoy her. But once she learned of Bim's family history, and all he'd been through with Hank, she'd quickly learned patience and a good bit of empathy for Bim.

So she'd started chatting with him about their cases, strictly business, although the way Bim had reacted to her attention at first had made Marly feel like she was being a flirt. But that was in the early days, when she was only working for Hank part-time, and they'd held their impromptu Finders, Incorporated meetings at the library, Hank's old apartment, or Panera Bread, just the four of them. Long before Afghanistan and the kids.

Marly smiled at the memory now, feeling nostalgic for that time, even though she knew it had been tough going. There were a lot of weeks where Hank hadn't been able to pay her and Juan on time, and she'd had to pick up extra work waiting tables at Coyote Kitchen, and Juan had to go back to working the electronics department at Kmart. For a while there, back in the mid-nineties right after she and Juan got hitched, it looked like Finders, Inc. wasn't going to make it.

And then something had *changed*. Like a switch was thrown, and the Hankster and Bim had started finding more missing people. The cases started rolling in, getting solved, and generating profits as a result.

Marly was pretty sure that the change had been Bim. Hank did his damnedest to hide it and protect his big friend's skills, but Marly was on to them. They'd solved impossible cases and found people who had been impossible to find. Unless they had some kind of help. Something more than just Bim's amazing connections and knowledge of the area—many of their cases took them off the mountain, for one—and something more than just Hank's uncanny ability to connect the dots that had been invisible to everyone else up until that point. And there were some people that she and Juan hadn't been able to track down with computers and phone calls and research.

It was like Bim and Hank just plucked these missing people out of thin air. Marly had been trying for almost twenty years to find out their secrets, but like most folks up here in the small mountain communities, they liked to keep their secrets tightly buried in the rocky ground of their psyches.

"Ooh," she said, tapping her phone a few times to open a new audio file. She repeated "secrets tightly buried in the rocky ground of their psyches" into her phone and tapped the Save button. "Nice one," she congratulated herself.

She set the Slocumb file off to the far right-hand corner of her desk and went through the rest of the two dozen files over the course of the next hour. She never had to pick up her phone to record more notes, however. Not even a single text from Juan, either, which made her want to text him, just to see how it was coming. She'd wait to power on her laptop again when she got his all-clear.

The other potential cases, all of which Hank and Bim hadn't had time to deal with in the past few weeks, had nothing to do with drugs or even any missing persons, much less retired college profs. Just a bunch of divorce cases, some OSHA cases, a few favor cases digging up evidence for lawyer friends, and one case involving a suspected dog-fighting ring.

"Poor pups," Marly said, closing the file on a dozen photos of injured and maimed Rottweilers and pit bulls.

She grabbed her phone and held it up, but didn't tap the screen.

Hank and Shelby can do their private-eye stuff on their own, she thought. And I don't need to get Bim involved here. I can do the detective work on my own. Just watch me.

She didn't want to admit it to herself, but Marly had felt more than a little burned when she saw Hank head over to Shelby's office after their lunch-time meeting today. The sound of Shelby's door closing behind Hank had felt like the door closing on Marly's career.

Marly had been tempted to record that line into her phone's app, but the sound of it was way too depressing.

But now that she'd had time to cool off and find some leads of her own, she hit Record again.

"First order of business: get in touch with Douglas Slocumb's wife, and talk to Mr. Slocumb himself, too, if I can. Then one of us should talk to those three App State kids about their visit to the hospital. We need to find out who their meth suppliers were. And figure out why the hell they'd want to use that stuff, anyway. Whatever happened to college kids drinking booze and smoking pot?"

Marly tapped Save on her phone again and checked the time. Almost three p.m. She still had plenty of daylight to do set up some visits before the day was over.

Leaving the Slocumb case on her desk, she carried the others over to Shelby's office. She leaned forward before knocking, hoping to get a hint of what they were discussing in there, but the big wooden office door blocked all but the low buzzing of first Hank's voice, then Shelby's.

They were chatting away in there like old friends already, Marly noted. She ignored her rising frustration and hints of jealousy and knocked on the door.

Hank answered a heartbeat later.

"Marly," he said. "Come on in!"

"I've got the files from the cases we haven't gotten to yet," she said as she stepped into the warm office. The door closed behind her. "I thought I'd hand these off to you guys."

Hank started to reach for them, then stopped.

"Can you go through these, Shelby? See if there's anything that might be related to the Holhouser case or the meth cases? You never know, your theory about all of this being connected might be on the right track."

Marly passed the files to Shelby, who thanked her. She didn't bother mentioning that she'd already done just that.

Watch me, she thought again.

"Sure," Shelby said, her voice neutral. "I'll take a look. But I thought we were going to check out the various nursing homes this afternoon..."

"Yeah," Hank said, scratching his chin-beard absently. "I think Bim and I should go do that, actually. Just... well, just because."

Marly looked from Hank to Shelby in an awkward silence. She knew she should've said something about the Slocumb case, but at that moment she didn't want to speak up. Hank had been complaining about being overworked and needing help, and here he was with a new employee who wanted to work, but he wasn't letting her.

"So, yeah, I've got some copies to make," Marly said. She turned on her heel, opened the door, and walked out of the office.

Let them have their power struggle, she thought. I've got the wife of a potentially wrongly imprisoned man to talk to.

Back in the lobby, she inhaled the musty air of the old hotel, part of her regretting her abrupt exit, but the rest of her glad to be out of that too-warm office. She glanced through the glass front door at Bim's outside office, and noticed he had put up a black-and-white DO NOT DISTURB sign on the metal door leading to his six-sided lair.

Probably napping in there, again. Lucky.

But before she hooked up with Douglas Slocumb's wife, she had to check on her own spouse. As she approached Juan's office, she could feel the cool air slipping out of his office and hear the hum of the servers firing on all cylinders again.

Perfect, she thought. I can fire up my laptop again and do some more research—

Before she could finish that thought, the alarm for the hotel began blaring all over again. And Juan was swearing in Spanish in his office as the hum of the servers abruptly ended.

Marly did a one-eighty and headed back to her office with a growing sense of dread. She did *not* need to be around Juan right now. And she did not need to think about who might want to inflict this kind of damage on them. She hoped it was just a random attack, but something told her this was something a bit more personal.

She went back to her office to get her phone. But before dialing anyone, she walked over to the front doors to watch the snow falling outside.

This winter was never going to end, she thought, watching the traffic on 321 creep past below her. And I've got to go out in that mess soon to pick up the kids from the after-school program. Definitely don't want Mom driving in this snow to go get them.

Feeling time ticking away, she walked back to her office, ignoring the banging sounds coming from Juan's office, and closed the door so she could call Janice, Douglas Slocumb's wife.

But when she lifted her phone to make the call, the rectangular screen was black, and there was nothing she could do to get the thing to work. Despite all of Juan's safeguards, the hackers had gotten to her phone now, too.

She let out a shaky breath. Finders, Inc., was pretty much dead in the water right now.

Chapter Nine

*This batch was coming together just as planned. The stink of ammonia burned the inside of her nose if she got too close to the cooker, but the right mix of heat and ingredients and careful—*very *careful!—stirring would pull the whole thing together. She felt an equal mix of fear and giddiness at what she was doing, but when all was said and done, the best thing about this was how she felt gloriously* useful *again.*

She turned off the heat and set the pot to one side to cool. Out of habit she straightened things, putting away the various ingredients, wanting things to look just so when her new boss came by to inspect. As always, she didn't look too closely at any of the bottles or canisters of ingredients. Instead she walked past the unlocked door leading outside and went over to the lone window once more.

She didn't want to move the towel. Something about looking outside filled her with dread. But the days' work had made her confident, and she'd made her quota for the first time since her arrival here, so she reached for the towel. Her hand looked small and frail with its liver spots and pale white skin, but this time she managed to use that hand to move the towel out of the way.

A face was looking in from the outside at her.

She nearly cried out and let go of the towel. Then she realized (of course!) that it was full dark out there already, and she was gazing at her own reflection. Her long white hair was slightly disheveled—something she quickly fixed with her free hand—and her eyes had dark half-circles under them. She looked tired and definitely a bit surprised, and yet there was a youthful energy to her face as well. She couldn't deny that.

This could help him with his early-onset dementia, she thought. It could halt it in its tracks. She'd read the pamphlet over and over until it started to fall apart. The science made sense.

As her eyes adjusted to the dark outside, she could just barely see the evergreens that surrounded the property to her left. To her right was the outline of the old house where nobody lived anymore. She squinted up there, trying to determine if anything was going on inside. Then she was blinded by the lights of a four-wheeled ATV as it turned toward this little building. She dropped the towel again, hands shaking.

The engine grew louder, and she moved back to her work area to check the finished product as it crystallized in the pot. This had to be the right consistency. Her new boss had given her the recipe and materials; it was up to her to make it all work.

Despite the strangeness of this situation, and the headlong way it had all come about, she was having more fun *here than she'd ever had before in her life.*

* * * * *

Bim opened his eyes with a gasp. He was on his side on the old couch in his outdoor office, and Delia Holhouser's earrings and pen had dropped from his numb hand onto the dusty floor. He was smiling even as his heart beat madly in his chest.

At some point the light had drained out of the day. The three window-walls of his poolside office were now mirrors, and he wasn't crazy about what he saw reflected in them. He groaned and rolled painfully to a sitting position, glancing at himself just for a moment in the windows. He looked a mess, but he was used to that look.

On the far wall, this former pool room had a huge, completely illogical mural depicting Adam and Eve on the far left, and a Dick and Jane couple from the '70s on the far right. The way in which the mural had transitioned between the two eras was so disturbing that Bim had immediately covered up the entire wall with flattened cardboard boxes he'd tacked up to hide the images from his vision.

The details of his connection to Delia slowly came back to him as he stared at his wild hair and scraggly beard in the cooling air of his office. She'd looked healthy and strangely happy when she'd taken a good look at her own reflection, and Bim felt pretty sure it had been a simultaneous connection—that what he saw was happening right now, no time delay.

He just couldn't figure out *where* the hell she was. She wasn't in some room in someone's house, but in a kind of shed. Surrounded by pine trees. With the main house about a hundred yards away, hidden in the darkness.

"Crap," he said. "That could be just about *any* place outside around here."

He needed more information, but Delia hadn't wanted to cooperate. He closed his eyes, thinking that there was *something* there, some detail he could use to find her. His scalp was itching, which usually happened when he was close to putting his finger on something.

Or maybe I just need a shower so I can wash my hair, he thought as he opened his eyes again in defeat. He'd lost that brief feeling of familiarity he'd had with the setting of Delia's meth lab.

"Who knows if that's even what she's cooking there," he muttered. He bent down to grab the earrings and pen once more. He had to reach and reach around his belly to get there. "Maybe she's just making some cake batter or frosting or something."

Instead of wallowing in frustration, though, Bim had to grin. He'd made his best connection yet with Delia just now, after trying to do so for most of the day. He hadn't lost his ability to reach other people, after all. He just couldn't figure out how Delia had gotten involved in this, because it sure *looked* like she was cooking up meth in that little white shed.

But that was all *motive*, which was Hanky J's area, not his. Bim just needed to find her and get her back home safe.

With another groan and a good bit of effort, he got himself up from the couch at last. His head swam with the sudden change in altitude, along with the emptiness in his belly. He wondered what was going on back inside the office. He also wondered if there was any pizza left over.

When this case is done, he reassured himself as he stood next to his messy desk and scratched his belly, I'll get back to eating right and exercising more.

Bim didn't want to go home, even though nearly everyone else had left the premises now that it was six thirty. The last time he'd checked, Juan had still been in his office, working away at his hacked servers, with all the phones and laptops for the Finders folks stacked on his desk like so many bricks. None of them were working, and Bim felt a twinge of anxiety when he felt his sweatpants pocket and didn't touch his phone.

Juan had probably told Marly to go home, while Hanky J and Shelby had left in Hanky J's crappy Escort about two hours ago. Bim had begged off from that trip, not wanting to go visit any old-folks homes today, even if they did contain a lead or two.

Instead he chose to stay out in his cold office, inhaling the metallic stink of his overworked space heaters, and tried to make one last connection with Delia Holhouser before he called it quits for the day. This had been his fifth attempt to reach her, and now that he'd finally connected with her, he could feel a migraine the size of Elk Knob Mountain coming on.

Massaging his temples with a chubby hand, Bim thought about his college-aged neighbors back at his apartment complex, and how they were all probably prepping to go out and hit the dance clubs downtown to start the weekend early this Thursday night. Just kids, all of them half his age, going out to cut loose and be stupid and try new things.

And some of those kids were going to try this new meth moving through town, just on a dare most likely. And a couple of them might not survive the night. Maybe some of the meth they'd try would be meth that Delia Holhouser had helped cook up in that white-walled shed. Somewhere up on a mountain.

Yes! Bim thought as he smacked his own stubbly cheek. She was somewhere up high.

He knew that now. Having lived on a mountain all his life, he knew what kind of view a mountain house had. Maybe it was the height of the trees that he'd glimpsed through that otherwise-towel-covered window. Or something in the way things felt when he slipped into Delia's head. The weight of the air, or something.

Bim opened his bear paw to look at the earrings and chewed-on pen once again.

I should try to connect to her one more time, he thought. See who was on that four-wheeler, and get a good look at the house.

But his head hurt, his empty stomach ached, and it was getting too chilly to stay out here.

He dug around the mess on top of his desk until he found his battered blue tablet. He was supposed to bring this to Juan for virus-cleansing, but he hadn't been able to find it until now. He tapped the screen, wanting to open a browser so he could pull up a map of the area, but the screen remained blank. It refused to turn on.

Crystal *meth*, he thought, staring at the black screen. There was no such thing when we were teenagers—not up here, at least. What high schooler or college kid would think *snorting* that shit would be a good idea?

Distracted, Bim began straightening up the papers and folders on his desk, and then he moved over to the random piles of junk stacked in the corner of his new office: broken lawn chairs, pool-cleaning tools, a smelly plastic container of Clorox that he picked up and set outside in the fresh snow, far from his door. Soon, by a quarter to eight, Bim had his office straight, and Juan still hadn't left.

Bim walked out of his own office and trudged out into the snow to see what Juan had gotten accomplished. The front of the building was dark, and he imagined a big, bright sign up there with a sleek Finders, Inc. logo emblazoned on it.

Soon, he thought.

Back inside the old hotel lobby, he found the last two slices of Hungry Howie's pizza in the break room. He thought for a belly-rumbling moment about just downing them both, but then he had a change of heart and brought the box with the second slice with him to Juan's office. The first one he inhaled in three bites.

He found Juan resting his forehead on the flat, now-empty surface of his desk. Bim almost stepped back away from the chilly office, but he wanted to check to make sure Juan was still breathing before he retreated.

"Yo," Bim called out, and Juan jumped and sat up fast. "Got the last piece of Howie's for ya, bro."

"Damn," Juan said. "Scared the crap out of me, man. Why you still here?"

Bim shrugged and tossed the box onto Juan's desk.

"How's the virus-killing and malware-busting going?"

Juan grabbed the last slice and took a huge bite.

"Not good. Someone knows their shit, and they used all the tricks in their book to blow us out of the water. I can't even get to Google from any of these," he said, gesturing at the various laptops, tablets, and phones spread out around the room, on pretty much every flat surface but Juan's empty desk. All of them had cables running from them to one of the desktop computers. To Bim they looked like patients with IVs in the electronics intensive care unit.

"So I guess no marathon games on the Atari console tonight, eh?" Bim said. He flipped through the tablets and phones around the office until Juan stopped him with a withering look. "Sorry. So have you got a lead on where they're from? Or who they are?"

"It's at least two different people from up north, possibly New York City, but it could be New Jersey. Not Delaware or Idaho like I'd originally thought. And someone from outside the country altogether. Maybe Africa, maybe Russia."

"Get outta here," Bim said with a sudden chill, regretting asking for any details.

Those folks from all around the world were probably combing through all our data now, he thought. Hope they don't hit *my* online browsing history.

"They did a nice job covering their own butts, and they've kept me too busy dealing with server issues, so I can't *track* the bastards." Juan smacked his desk. "We really should've moved all this to a secure data center. It's my fault for not doing that sooner, damn it."

Bim suddenly wished Hanky J was here, because staring at that dead hardware made him think of all the information that could be lost from all those drives. All those cases.

"Think it's related to any of our current cases?" he asked Juan. "Like this meth stuff?"

Juan shrugged, looking annoyed at the distraction. If it didn't directly have to do with fixing their stuff, he probably didn't care. Bim understood that.

"So can I help with anything?" Bim said, licking his fingers and wishing he had another two or four slices of pizza. "I got time."

"It's all *just* a matter of time now. Need to let these cleaning programs and scripts run. Then I'm going to take a virtual trip to this asshole hacker's house and wreck *his* life as a reward."

"Dude," Bim said, and then he stopped. He knew better than to push Juan when he was in a mood like this. "Want me to close the office door behind me when I leave?"

Juan's only answer was a shrug.

He left Juan's office feeling suddenly exhausted. He wished he knew more about fixing hacked hardware, but he was a point-and-click guy only. He liked learning how to *use* the stuff, but didn't dare try getting his fat fingers entangled in the wiring and guts of a server like Juan was able to do. And forget trying to figure out code—he'd made it maybe four weeks in a programming class at App State before dropping that class like it was hot.

He could see snow falling again outside the front doors. He stopped under the chandelier, not wanting to freeze his fingers, toes, and nose off outside in his office any longer. He patted his pocket and felt Delia's earrings and pen again.

Instead of taking another step forward, he simply dropped onto one of the overstuffed arm chairs below the chandelier and took a deep breath, willing to risk Juan witnessing his attempts to reach out for Delia once more.

He and Hanky J had promised each other they'd never tell Juan or Marly or anyone else about his abilities. As an outsider all his life, Bim usually didn't care much what people thought, but when it came to his secret way of connecting with people, he didn't want anyone but Hanky J to know. It was just too damn strange.

But before he could wrap his hand around Delia's earrings and pen and close his eyes, Bim saw a person scurry past the front doors.

Bim gripped the handrests to the chair, ready to pull himself up and out, but he didn't have the energy to chase down the intruder.

It was probably Bill or Pops, two of the homeless guys who spent most of their days panhandling in front of Walmart—which to Bim was one of the dumbest places to ask for handouts, as most of the poorer people in the county relied on the Mart for groceries and clothes, so they wouldn't have a hell of a lot of cash left over for grungy guys holding signs full of misspellings about their plights. But Bim liked talking to them whenever he ran into them around town, although Bill was downright crazy, and Pops was always slightly sad as he dispensed mostly worthless advice about the stock market and football.

If Bill or Pops wanted to hole up in one of the rooms here and get out of the cold and snow, Bim had absolutely no problem with it. He understood that Marly was creeped out by the idea, but she didn't know these guys like Bim did.

He made another, more determined attempt to get up out of his chair, and this time it worked. He'd flick off the alarm so Bill or Pops could slip into one of the rooms for the night. Bim's headache had receded, at last, and as he walked over to the alarm to disarm it, he felt what just might have been a second wind.

I should check on Delia H one more time, he thought as he reached for the alarm. I think I might be able to recognize where—

But before he could either finish that thought or type in the pass code on the glowing blue keypad, the alarm began to blare all over again.

Hands over his ears, Bim used the glow of lights from down below in the city to charge out of the lobby, into the snow, and into the safety and relative silence of his six-sided office once more.

Sorry to leave you with that, Juan, he thought as he dropped onto the old couch with huge puff of dust. But I forgot the password already.

Ears ringing, with one hand in the pocket of his sweat pants, Bim closed his eyes.

* * * * *

And this time he saw what he needed to see.

He'd connected to Delia just as she was getting ready to try one more combination of ingredients, and run it through the cooker again. She felt like she couldn't leave the place, even though they'd never had to lock the doors with her. There was just so much to learn, and so much to do.

When she stepped out of the door that night, after a good twenty minutes of fiddling and mixing that had felt like twenty hours to Bim, she walked out into a forest of pines and maples. Sixty and seventy-footers, at least, Bim estimated. The light was gone, but he could tell they were high up and far from town based on the completeness of the dark. Barely any light pollution up there.

Bim felt a growing tickle in his hind-brain. This place. He'd been here before. He shuddered, but didn't know why.

And then he saw the house. It was a huge, rambling thing in the darkness, blotting out the stars as Delia picked her way up the dirt trail leading from the shacks—not just one shack, Bim noted, but four. The house was two stories, with a round window in the attic, and it leaned precariously toward Delia as she approached it. Runaway rhododendron bushes were trying to take over the wraparound porch, and it was the bushes that had distracted Bim initially.

Those bushes hadn't been there when he was a kid, visiting his Uncle Harry.

Bim had broken the connection with Delia and found himself on the floor of his office. He'd rolled right off the couch.

He let go of the earrings and the pen in his pocket so he could put both hands over his face and wait for his pulse to go back to normal. As he sucked in one deep, shaky breath after another, he did a mental check to make sure that this was the place he'd feared it was.

Was the house he'd seen really the same house? The lights had been off, so she couldn't have been staying there. And it couldn't have gotten that run down in the twenty-five years since he was there last. Uncle Harry hadn't lived there in over a decade, not since he and Aunt Annie had split up. Bim had always figured that Harry and Annie had sold the place, which was just half a mile down the road from Dad's house—he called it his "ranch"—at the very top of Mayer Mountain. And Harry hadn't had all those shacks on the property, back in the day.

Bim rubbed his bare arms and paced around his little office.

I've got to verify this, he thought, and then paused in his pacing. He was quickly losing his sense of urgency with this mission. No, *Hanky J* needs to verify this. He's the one with the license and the know-how. I'm just the finder guy. And I'm not even sure this is the right place.

Bim cracked open the door leading outside and listened. Juan had gotten the alarm back off, fortunately, which enabled Bim to hear the soft patter of hard snow falling, along with the distant rumble of a car or two down on 321. Already partially hidden in the snow were the prints from Bim's flip-flops, which intersected with the scuffling, slightly uneven footsteps left by the intruder earlier that night. Those footsteps headed off to Bim's left, disappearing around the corner of the last room on that end of the hotel. To the right, a good fifty feet away, sat Juan's customized car—he always ignored the handicapped spots, on principle.

Bim smacked his forehead. He had no transportation. Hanky J had picked him up early this morning, way too early for Bim's taste, because of the interview Hanky J had scheduled with Miranda. He wanted Bim along for the ride, just in case Miranda needed a quote from Hanky J's trusty fat sidekick.

Bim reached for his phone and smacked his forehead again. Juan still had all the phones in his office, of course. And they were all dead.

Instead of going back inside the building to bother Juan again, Bim went into his office to dig through his desk for change. There was a pay phone at the Walgreen's just down the hill from here.

Mom will be so proud of me, Bim thought as he grabbed a sweatshirt from a nail on the wall and headed out into the snowy night. Finally calling Dad to see how he's doing. And interrogating him about his brother's old house and property as well. Two birds, one stone.

Chapter Ten

Shelby had lived in the big city for so long that she'd just assumed all coffee shops were now owned by Starbucks and other corporations instead of actual people. But here she was at the Local Lion, ordering a medium vanilla latte and inhaling the intoxicating smells of roasted coffee and fresh-made donuts, without a trace of the corporate anywhere. This place was filled with sunlight, casual, and hip, and she'd be hard-pressed to find a better place to meet up with Janice Slocumb.

Today marked the end of her first, shortened week at Finders, Incorporated, but she was in no way ready to relax into the weekend. Not with all these cases and leads falling onto her lap, and especially not with today's newspaper in her hand, reporting *another* meth-related story—this one about a bust at an off-campus party on the southern edge of town.

I got hired on here just in time, she thought as the cappuccino machine let off a loud hiss as the barista steamed milk for Shelby's drink. This town and the surrounding area are coming apart at the seams.

She grabbed a seat at the otherwise empty cafe under the building's exposed beams, a few tables away from the monstrous green roaster parked in the corner of the window-filled sitting area. She'd had to cut it short with the bubbly, already-caffeinated female barista. The girl made a mean latte, Shelby acknowledged, but after chatting with two dozen old folks and a dozen nurses and aides until late last night with Hank, she was a bit talked out. Maybe all she needed was a good dose of caffeine.

Ten minutes later, Shelby had read all about the meth bust as well as the rest of the ad-filled paper, and then she opened her slim black Moleskine notebook and read over her handwritten notes on the case, twice. She would've preferred using her new tablet, which already had three pages of notes on it, but it remained down for the count back at the office. Hank had given her half a dozen other minor cases as well, but none of them had grabbed her attention like the meth and the missing professors cases. Or maybe they were all part of one big case, as she was starting to seriously suspect.

Shelby downed the last of her drink with regret, wishing she'd gotten a large instead of medium. While she waited for the buzz to kick in, and for Janice to arrive, she watched traffic drive past as bundled-up students hoofed it through the slush and snow to their early-morning classes. Almost all the vehicles on the road were hefty four-wheel drive SUVs and pickups, with lots of Subaru wagons thrown in for good measure.

She'd gotten a call from Marly late last night on her cell phone—which luckily hadn't been hit by the hacker attack at the Finders HQ yesterday. Her new co-worker had sounded very harried and especially tired on the other end of the line.

"I've got to apologize to you," Marly had said before Shelby could even attempt any small talk. "I would've called sooner, but my kids took forever to get to bed, and Juan still hasn't made it home from the office."

"You don't need to apologize for that—"

"Oh, just wait. Here's the thing. I've been holding onto some information that I should've shared with you and Hank. I thought I could go rogue and do this myself, but the thought of meeting up with her tomorrow scares the snot out of me. She was a bit, um, *intense* on the phone. So I need your help."

"Okay," Shelby had said, trying to piece together the various lines of Marly's wandering monologue. "Who is 'she'? And when are you meeting with her tomorrow?"

So Marly had told her all about Janice Slocumb, the local woman whose husband Douglas had been in and out of jail over the past decade for running meth. And how this last time, when Douglas got his third sentence for five years, Janice had come to the Finders to get them to investigate.

"She swears he was set up this last time," Marly said. "That his lawyer didn't even put up a fight or try to do some sort of plea deal. She's adamant about this even now. I just talked to her on the phone ten minutes ago." Marly let took a loud, shuddering breath. "She's so *calm* about it. But I can tell she's really, really mad, too. It shook me. So can you do this for me? Please?"

"Marly," Shelby said, having already filled up a page in her Moleskine and starting another. "What is it you want me to do?"

"Oh," Marly said. She let out a nervous laugh. "I'm not usually this scattered, okay? Sorry. But I went ahead and told Janice Slocumb I'd meet with her tomorrow for coffee at the Local Lion. She has to make it to her shift at Walmart by eight thirty, so I told her I'd be there at seven a.m., sharp. Could *you* meet her for me, explain that I couldn't make it? And then talk to her for me?"

Grimacing at the thought of getting up that early, Shelby had agreed to do it, without suggesting that Marly call the woman back to reschedule it herself. Who knew what kind of impression Marly had made on the phone with the woman already, and she'd already gotten the cold shoulder from the company earlier. But people who felt like they'd been wronged by the system were usually persistent, so Shelby knew Janice wouldn't mind talking to her even if she was expecting to talk to Marly.

She wouldn't mind, that was, if she ever showed up today.

As the minutes crept closer to seven thirty, and a handful of people had come inside to grab coffee and donuts, none of them so much as glancing at Shelby, she began to get irritated. She'd been up until one a.m. last night, writing down all her notes from their chats with the people from the various old folks home, and she'd been planning on waking up about this time, instead of losing a good two hours of sleep.

There had been a lot of irrelevant information in their interviews, a bunch of old folks complaining about the food and the long therapy sessions and the rude nurses, but she and Hank had learned of the disappearance of one other resident from one of the homes—a disappearance that the administrators of the home had managed to keep hushed up until Hank pried the information out of them. That had happened over four weeks ago, in mid-February, and the missing old guy's name was Webster Ashley. He also was a retired Chemistry professor. They'd raided the whole department, it seemed. Whoever *they* were.

In addition, two nurses from Glenbridge Health had noticed a tall black man in his late thirties or so, chatting with Delia Holhouser on a visit with her husband James a week before she'd disappeared.

Hank had grilled the nurses about that, and he'd gotten a pretty good, consistent description of the guy. Shelby suspected that they didn't get a lot of black people in the home for visits, so they'd both taken notice. Hank had mentioned how he'd gotten the stink-eye from the nurse at Glenbridge earlier that day, so it made sense that they were suspicious.

After that little bit of evidence, Hank's mood had soured, and they'd wrapped up all their interviews ten minutes later. Judging from his reaction, Shelby was pretty sure Hank knew the guy. This could quite likely have been the "thug fellow" that James had mentioned to her yesterday, before Hank had barged in to take over the situation. She closed her notebook with a caffeine-shaky hand.

I'll give Janice fifteen more minutes, she told herself, and then I'm out of here. I've got way too much work to do to sit around a coffee shop waiting on a junkie felon's wife.

To make the wait more bearable, she got up and asked the barista for a fresh mug of their Sumatra blend.

"Gluten-free Friday," the still-perky, bespectacled girl behind the counter reminded Shelby. "We finally got the recipe right. I actually like 'em better than the gluten-filled ones nowadays. Here, try a maple donut, on the house."

"No, I shouldn't," Shelby said, thinking about those last few pounds she couldn't get rid of.

"Life is short," the barista laughed. "And the donuts are still hot."

"Okay, you twisted my arm," Shelby said, picking up the still-warm donut along with her fresh, steaming mug. She took a bit, thinking about Blake Barham, along with Delia and James Holhouser. Life was *indeed* short. And the donut was warm and delicious.

"Can't believe those kids were snorting meth at that party last night," the barista said, waving her copy of the paper in the air. She seemed determined to keep Shelby at the counter to chat. "My younger sister knew a couple of 'em. Dumb butts. They're lucky they got caught now, before they get addicted and start losing their teeth and their hair and dropping outta college. I've seen that happen to—"

Shelby had her back to the front door, so she couldn't see who had just walked in and stopped the barista in mid-sentence.

A small woman wearing dark blue pants, a white T-shirt, and a too-thin denim coat walked in the door. She had thin black hair streaked with gray that went down past her shoulders, and her narrow face looked stuck in a permanent frown.

Shelby made a mental note to pick up the meth-related conversation again with the barista as she moved away from the counter.

"Janice?" she asked the newly arrived woman. A wave of cold, snowy air followed the too-thin woman inside before she could pull the heavy wooden door closed behind her.

The woman gave a quick nod, all business.

"Marly, right?"

Shelby gave her an apologetic smile. "Actually, I'm Shelby Jamiston. Marly got called away on some other business and couldn't make it. Can I buy you a coffee? Any kind, my treat."

Janice's brown eyes lightened for a moment, and then she looked over at the barista. A cloud crossed her face.

"No thanks," she said, her voice gravelly and low. "I don't much like the coffee here."

Despite wanting to, badly, Shelby didn't dare look behind her at the barista. Instead, she led Janice to the table farthest from the front counter, one that was partially hidden by the roaster. She felt too tall and lumbering next to Janice's short, compact movements.

"I called you guys over a *month* ago," Janice said without any emotion, just matter-of-fact, as soon as they sat down. "Never heard back. Guess we aren't as important as your other cases."

"We've been wanting to talk to you about your case for a while," Shelby began, hating how she sounded apologetic already. "But the agency has been a bit short-handed lately, and you probably know about some of the other cases we've been busy with."

Janice gave a quick nod.

"Well, we're here now," she said, "so let's talk. Douglas should *not* be in jail right now. Someone planted that meth on him. We've both been clean for almost three years." She leaned in closer, and Shelby caught sight of her yellowed teeth, just for the briefest of moments. "You know, we lost our *kids* because of meth. We been working hard to get them back. We're motivated now, you see? And then this happens, and we're *done*. Just done. No way we'll get our kids out of foster care now."

Shelby let Janice talk, jotting down the details in her notebook as fast as she could. She knew that clients found that reassuring, watching her take notes. And it gave her time to focus on the details, before getting hung up on the emotional angles of the situation.

"We're going to work on getting Douglas the help he needs," she said when Janice ran out of words and began to swipe angrily at her teared-up eyes. "I just need all the facts about the day he was picked up, and we'll build the case from there."

Janice nodded, pulling herself back together immediately.

"It was this construction crew he'd gotten hooked up with. Bunch of guys he knew from high school and community college over in Caldwell County. A couple of them were serious about getting good work and making some money, but there were some *other* laborers at the sites who got paid in cash and never showed up again the next week. Douglas knew they were smoking pot on the job or drinking from flasks when the boss guys weren't looking, so he kept his distance."

"Who owned the construction company?"

Janice shrugged and glanced back at the barista, who was welcoming two loud men in suits who'd just walked in.

"Augie Shepherd, the uncle of one of the serious guys. At least, it was Augie's name on the checks, and the checks Douglas brought home didn't bounce. But I don't think it was Augie that planted that meth on Douglas, even though that old fart has been up to all sorts of illicit crap in the past thirty or forty years. I think it was one of the drifter day laborers, wanting to get him fired. They didn't like him, thought he was a goody-goody. Just for trying to get ahead and stay clean."

Shelby finished writing and made a point of looking over what she wrote before turning her attention back to Janice. She doubted the day laborers would have enough cash to plant that much meth on Douglas to get him sent to jail for intent to distribute. But this *Augie* guy and his crew...

"Can you tell me the names of the men on the crew?"

Shelby wrote down the five names as fast as Janice said them, and made a note that there were two more men Janice couldn't remember.

"So the day Douglas got in trouble—what happened? How did the cops get involved?"

"They were adding on to this rich guy's house over on App Ski Mountain, and for some reason a pair of Boone cops show up on-site. Said the rich guy had been complaining about stuff going missing from his house recently, and they wanted to check things over with the crew. I know that mountain ain't even their jurisdiction—shoulda been the Blowing Rock police handling this. But the Boone cops got permission from James, the site supervisor and Augie Shepherd's nephew, to go through the cars of all the workers. James knew the cop, and he said he was confident his men wouldn't steal. So of course, they go to check Douglas's truck right off the bat, and they find a fucking *pound* of crystal meth in a Ziploc bag in his glove compartment. A pound. Douglas wouldn't do that, not anymore. He wanted to kill himself that night, but he didn't because of Zachary and Diane. Our kids. They're eight and five. All I know is, someone wanted him off that job, bad. Maybe he pissed off the wrong person. But nobody listened to a word he said. His lawyer got paid off, we know it. And Douglas is now seventeen days into a five-year sentence. Our kids won't know who he is when he gets out."

Shelby tapped her pen on her notebook, thinking. She needed to talk to Hank about this Augie Shepherd character, and then talk things over with the Boone cops who made the bust. She grimaced, thinking that Juan would've uncovered any missing details during his computer research, but all the computers had been hosed yesterday afternoon.

The hackers were slowing them down by at least half a day now, if not more.

"So?" Janice said. She'd caught the face that Shelby had made, along with the long silence.

"Just thinking over some issues we had at our office yesterday that just might be related. But that's neither here nor there. Tell me anything else you know that *you* think might be related. Any other people he might have interacted with, any strange behaviors he might have had, any unique incidents he might've been involved in or witnessed?"

Janice went silent, gazing down at Shelby's half-empty coffee. Shelby studied the other woman, noting her neatly clipped fingernails, her sparse makeup, and her thin, worn jacket. This wasn't the look of a meth user, or the wife of a meth user—so long as she didn't smile too widely. No, this was someone working hard to pull her life together.

"I'll be right back," Shelby said, placing a hand on Janice's shoulder on her way back to the front counter. She got a heat-up on her coffee, and asked for another mug of coffee as well.

"Careful with that one," the barista said as she passed Shelby the new mug. "She's a bit of trouble. I mean, I don't want to butt in, but you're working with Hank now, right? That lady's husband is in jail, and she's got some substance abuse issues, and some reality issues."

Shelby stared at the barista, who couldn't have been thirty. Probably closer to twenty-five, if that. She didn't know which question or accusation to address first, so she just gave the girl three one-dollar bills and walked away with her coffees.

"Here you go," Shelby said as she gave the barista one last disapproving glare and handed Janice the other coffee. Janice jumped, surprised out of her thoughts. "I don't know if you take cream or sugar or anything like that...?"

Janice grinned at her with her crooked, slightly yellowed teeth. Her eyes lost the dark-cloud look for the first time.

"Hey, no. This is fine. Thanks!"

"Anything else you want to share before we both have to hustle off to work?"

Janice took such a long gulp of coffee that Shelby felt her jaw almost drop. How the woman didn't burn her mouth and throat was beyond her.

"There was this one thing that Douglas told me about, three days before the setup. Back in February."

"Okay," Shelby said as she picked up her pen again. She forced herself to ignore the barista's comments about Janice having reality issues.

"Douglas was one of just three guys with a big enough truck bed to haul some deck stairs they were installing in the rich guy's house, so he drove to this old house they were tearing up to get 'em. He'd just loaded the stairs—all by himself, too, 'cause he didn't trust any of the other losers on the crew to go along and help him—when he saw smoke. He followed it up the mountain, up some steep gravel roads that he about slid off of, and he got about halfway down someone's gravel driveway when he saw the flames. It was this old shack, and he caught a whiff of the smell. A nasty smell, enough to make your eyes burn. It's a smell you don't forget. He backed the hell out of there, almost got stuck, but he thinks one of the guys putting out the fire saw him."

"Was it a meth lab?" Shelby asked, knowing the answer even before Janice nodded. "Where?"

"Middle of nowhere," Janice said, though she sounded a bit shaken all of a sudden. "One of those side roads you pass off the main road that say it's a private drive."

Shelby waited, then asked again, "Where?"

"Out past Boone on your way to Valle Crucis, past that fancy Hound Ears neighborhood off Shull's Mill Road, but before you get to Grandfather Mountain. Real close to Foscoe. Anyway, off to the left, there's mountains a few miles off the highway that are all secluded. I don't think anyone there saw Douglas that day, but you never know."

"I need to find this place," Shelby said, feeling more agitated by the moment, worried that Janice was caught in a lie and trying to spin her way out of it now. "On which mountain did Douglas see this fire?"

Janice drank the last of her coffee, chugging it like water. When she was done, she blinked hard enough to make tears slip from both eyes.

"The family that owns the mountain has been there forever. I don't want this getting back to me, okay?"

Shelby nodded, ignoring Janice's squirming, and closed her notebook.

"They call it Mayer Mountain. That's where Douglas saw the meth lab burning. Three days later, he was on his way to jail, again."

"Mayer Mountain," Shelby said as she tapped absently on her notebook, and then she dropped her pen.

I've got to talk to my new co-worker, she thought, a Mr. Bim *Mayer*, about this mountain.

Chapter Eleven

At eight o'clock on Friday morning, two days after finding April Mae, and less than a day after learning about Delia Holhouser, Hank found himself staring at five different phones spread out on his desk: three cells and two old-school land line phones. None of them were the same brand, none of them worked consistently, and none of them was his phone.

"So *when* is Marly supposed to get in?" he called from his office over to Juan, just as the middle phone—the one actually plugged into the jack in the wall—began to trill. Hank glared at it and waited for Juan to answer his question.

"Around 9," Juan called, his voice barely carrying across the lobby. "No later than 10!"

"*Great*," Hank muttered, and he picked up the phone on its fourth annoying trill.

This call was a young woman looking for a guy she'd met at a bar last week whose number she'd accidentally deleted from her phone. Hank listened to her story for as long as he could stand it before telling her as politely as possible, through clenched teeth, that she should go to the Missed Connections page on the Boone Craigslist or Match.com instead.

"This isn't the damn Love Connection," he growled at the phone after ending the call. He didn't know how Marly did it. Everyone had heard of Finders, Inc. thanks to the April Mae case, but it was the wrong kind of attention. Very few of the people contacting them had viable cases. It was like nobody truly understood what kind of work they did here.

And Hank had plenty of legitimate work to do on this case alone, not even counting the half dozen other cases he needed to finish up as well. There were notes to go over from all their interviews at the nursing homes yesterday, and more people to talk to about meth and missing professors.

He also had a voicemail from Charles that he needed to listen to, but he couldn't get his phone to work long enough to listen to it. Juan had fixed the servers late last night, though there was a good bit of corruption he was now dealing with. Marly usually handled the phones, routing all five phones to her single line, but she was out on kid- and school-related business, and the phone lines were still hosed. He knew he was supposed to cut Marly some slack, but her timing was terrible.

He peeked out into the lobby, hoping that Shelby might be arriving, or even Bim, so he could coerce one of them to take over the secretarial duties.

Hank pulled out the paper files he'd found on Marly's desk and added them to his own set of working files. In a way, he'd been glad to not have any gadgets connecting him to the outside world. Then he didn't have to deal with texts from Mom, asking about his upcoming date tonight with "Miss Miranda" (as she called her) or telling him about how she'd set him up with yet another highly desirable single woman in the Watauga County area.

He was secretly hoping the date with Miss Miranda wouldn't take place, due to his job-related obligations. That girl, as pretty and smart as she was, could be *exhausting* in her competitiveness. They'd kept in touch over the years since college, but that neediness to be number one had curdled any attraction he might've had for her. She'd actually *asked* him yesterday how much he'd made last year. No way he was going to tell her that. She would've been shocked at how little it had been, after expenses. All his extra money went into the company and funding this place.

At least I gave her some good story material with Webster Ashley's situation, he thought. He was counting on her to follow up that lead about how the nursing home had covered up his disappearance, and tie off any loose ends related to the case with that crappy home.

Hank rubbed his sore eyes and picked up a new file folder he'd never touched before. Last night he'd slept for over six hours, which totally threw off his only-four-hours-a-night plan, and as a result he felt both groggy and grumpy. He gave the phones one last warning look before opening the file, daring any of them to ring.

Maybe this was a bad time to try to instill new habits, he thought with a yawn, and then started reading.

"Douglas Slocumb?" he muttered five seconds later, scanning the short write-up in the folder.

He remembered the case immediately, and he winced at his abrupt language on the sticky note attached to the file. I must've been up to my ears in work that day, he thought, trying to justify his reasoning for not following up with the Slocumbs. Now, after all the meth incidents from the past few days, including the bust just south of campus last night, it felt like a huge mistake on his part.

That was hindsight for you, he thought.

He had just stood up to go over to Juan's office and get him to dive into the Slocumb case when all five phones spread across his desk rang suddenly. Hank reached a hand toward them instinctively, but before they could ring again, the lights—along with all the power—in the Finders, Inc. headquarters went out.

* * * * *

Half an hour later, Hank sat out in the lobby under the chandelier, squinting through the weak sunlight at the paper notebook resting on top of the file folders on his lap. The power was still out, and Juan had gone outside to quote-unquote *get some fresh air*. Hank knew he was grabbing a cigarette, a habit Juan had kicked years ago, but occasionally returned to in moments of high stress.

There was just enough light coming through the glass doors and the three big windows around the lobby for Hank to continue working. The big room was gradually cooling off, however, so he figured he had another hour or so before the place got too cold to stick around.

Either Juan or the electric company would have this outage handled by then, he hoped. And he needed to be out of here by that point, anyway, tracking down leads on these crazy meth and missing persons cases.

He shuddered to imagine what Shelby must think of their setup, with the crashed hardware and the incessant alarm and now the power outage. He hadn't even had time to show her how to enter all her case notes into the home-brewed software program that Juan and Bim had set up years ago. So he had no idea what kind of progress she'd made, or even who else she'd been talking to. It was like the early '90s all over again, with no Internet, no laptops, and no cell phones.

A huge step backwards, Hank thought, feeling his irritation grow. He took a series of long, slow breaths to center himself again so he could focus on his notebook.

He'd forced himself to review his work for four other, unrelated cases before he'd had no choice but to return to the Delia Holhouser case. He couldn't avoid it.

So he flipped back to his notes from yesterday, feeling flabbergasted that the disappearance of Webster Ashley had been so completely covered up by the last nursing home they'd visited. But after looking around at the home's dirty floors and inhaling the scent of urine and too much bleach yesterday, Hank hadn't been too surprised.

Some people could go through life doing a shabby job and it didn't bother them. Some people had no pride.

Hank sighed.

And with the weather taking a turn for the worst in the past two weeks, he didn't hold out much hope for Mr. Barham's well-being. Unless someone had *taken* him somewhere, essentially busting him out of the nursing home.

But where? And who would do something like that?

Mr. Barham didn't have any relatives that lived in the area, and his wife had passed away last year. Maybe he had some old poker buddies who'd been blessed with better health than him, and they needed a fourth player for their tournaments.

Or maybe this black guy that the nurses had described—a tall guy, with close-cropped hair, neat mustache, a tiny soul chip below his lip, and a one-inch diagonal scar on his right cheek—had something to do with the disappearances.

Hank closed his notebook and then his eyes, picturing the scar on that guy's right cheek with a sour feeling in his gut.

It couldn't be him, coming back here after all these years. Not now.

With an effort, he did some quick calculating in the darkness behind his eyelids. The office was strangely quiet with Juan outside and all the machinery dead again. Hank fought the urge to nap for a few minutes, and instead snapped his fingers.

That's it, he thought. No wonder Mom has been texting me like crazy, trying to distract herself from April the 3rd, just six days from now. The anniversary of the day that Dad was killed. Thirty years ago. But surely *he* wouldn't come back for that. I should get Juan to do a search for his—

A flash of light and the sound of the front door opening interrupted Hank's thoughts. He felt the cold wind rush in, and he was about to call out to Juan to give him a hard time about backsliding with his cigs, but then he saw that it was actually Shelby walking in the door.

"The *power* went out?" she asked before the door could closer behind her. "No way."

Hank stood up and spread his arms wide apologetically.

"We're usually not in such a bad state as this," he said. "It was just a chain reaction, probably from the workload that Juan's servers were putting on the electrical system."

She nodded in a distracted fashion, looking around the lobby at the other offices with their closed doors.

"Where's everyone else?" she asked. "I passed Juan outside, freezing his butt off with a cancer stick, but I *really* need to talk to Bim."

"Marly's got kid stuff for the next hour or so." Hank checked his watch: 8:56 a.m. "And Bim's still sleeping at his apartment, most likely. He doesn't come in too early most days, but *especially* not on Fridays."

Shelby nodded, still standing in front of the glass doors, as if trying to make a decision.

"I know this has been a pretty crazy first week," Hank tried again as he walked towards her. She didn't seem to interested in stepping inside the office.

"Could you give me Bim's address?"

Hank stopped twenty feet from her. "Sure. Is everything all right?"

Shelby opened her mouth as if to say something, but then she reconsidered. She exhaled loudly, and Hank could see her breath clouding up in the cooling air of the lobby.

"I just really need him to confirm a few things," she said at last, and Hank knew he didn't need to pursue that anymore right now. Instead he gave her directions to Mossy Creek Apartments.

"Be careful when you turn off 321 onto the road leading up to the apartments," he said, waiting for her to write down the address on a piece of paper or into her phone, but she'd apparently memorized it. *Nice*. "They don't plow that road enough, so it's always slick. And watch the potholes. Oh, and you may not want to actually go *into* his apartment. It's usually a bit of a mess."

"I can handle myself," Shelby said with a fleeting grin. "Thanks. I'd better run over there now."

"Hold on a second," Hank said, a bit louder and sharper than he'd planned. "Can you give me an update on what you've learned so far? Any facts or details or theories?"

Shelby let out another steaming breath and zipped up her coat tight. The place was really cooling off now.

"There are some interesting nuances I haven't quite figured out yet," she said. "But it sounds like somebody, or maybe a *group* of somebodies, has been planning the return of meth to the area for the past few months. Things could get a lot worse in the coming weeks. I don't quite have a handle on the missing elderly people angle, or if that's at all related. I have a hunch it is. Could be your Breaking Bad theory is on the money, and these ringleaders really did snatch the old folks from their houses and the nursing homes."

Hank caught himself nodding along so fast his vision blurred. He'd been clenching his jaw closed tight to keep from interjecting while Shelby gave him her report.

"Also," Shelby added, "speaking of ringleaders, I did get a name: Augie Shepherd."

"Augie," Hank said, followed by a groan. If you knew him, you couldn't help but say his name like that: *Augie Ugh...*

"I know him, all too well. Scraggly old white guy in his sixties, always got his hand in half a dozen projects that usually turn out to be some sort of scam. Supposed be running his own construction crew, but half the time he's just using that as a front for his other activities. I'm not surprised he's connected to all this."

"He's definitely connected to the meth side of things. And maybe the missing professors thing, but I haven't figured out all the details yet."

Hank stepped closer. "You said *missing* professors," he said, "not kidnapped professors. So you're not sold on the kidnapping theory?" Hank nearly clapped his hands together when Shelby shook her head. "Me neither. Something feels off about it."

"Agreed. I mean, where would they..." Shelby trailed off as her eyes widened. "Crap. I *really* have to go, boss."

"Wait, what—"

She was backing up toward the front doors so fast Hank was worried she might trip and fall.

"Full report when I get back, I promise," she said.

And then with a puff of frigid air, she was out the door.

"You could just *call* Bim," Hank said to the empty, dark, and increasingly chilly lobby. "If we had a phone here that worked..."

As he watched Shelby drive away in her ridiculously big Crown Victoria, Hank realized too late that he should've ridden along with her to Bim's apartment, so they could all work together on this case, and hopefully close it down.

Before he could hurry out and follow Shelby to Bim's place in his car, Hank felt a sudden buzz from his pants pocket.

He pulled out his now-silent cell phone, which had been totally worthless all morning thanks to the hacker's handiwork. He had over a dozen texts waiting for him, ten of which were from Mom, and two from Miranda. Ignoring them, he saw that he'd missed another call from Charles, so he now had *two* new voicemails from the Boone detective.

The first one was from 6:41 a.m. that morning, and it was brief: "Johnson, give me a call when you get this message. Got some news for you."

That didn't sound good, Hank thought as he queued up the second voicemail from a few seconds ago.

"Johnson," Charles said in his gruff voice, "you gotta start answering your phone, or I'm gonna stop calling. Listen, there's been some new evidence in this case, thanks to last night's bust. The junk we got there matches all the other junk, but there's something new about it, too. Like a new recipe or something. Guys are checking the DNA on it right now. Gimme a call if you want more."

"A new recipe," Hank murmured, thinking about the missing Chemistry professors, and trying to figure out just what the heck Augie Ugh Shepherd was doing in the middle of all this.

The lights flickered on for a split-second, and the various fans for the heating tried to get started, and then the lights died and everything went silent again.

Juan came charging in from the cold a few seconds later.

"What was that?" he shouted. "Was that the power?"

Hank shook his head. "It tried to come back on, then *pbbbt.*"

Juan rolled past, smelling like smoke and giving off a wave of arctic cold that made the cool lobby feel like the tropics.

With a shiver, Hank lifted his phone again. He didn't want to have to deal with Charles this early in the morning, but it was obvious the guy had more info for him that he hadn't wanted to share in his voicemails.

Just as he was about to tap on Charles's number, though, another call popped up on his phone's screen. This looked like a real call that was actually going to come through.

It was an area code he didn't recognize, but he answered the call anyway.

"This is Hank," he said, wincing as the door to Juan's office slammed shut.

"*Bro*," a chuckling voice responded. "So good to hear your voice again!"

Hank felt a bone-deep chill that had nothing to do with the broken heat in his new headquarters.

"William," he said. "What are *you* up to?"

"About six foot one," his younger brother responded without hesitation. An old, old joke. Hank had six years on William, but William had six inches of height on Hank. "And I'm back in town again. Although I'll bet a sharp private eye like you already knew I was back."

Hank put a hand to his forehead, feeling his stress levels triple. Thirty years ago.

"How long are you back?"

William let loose another one of his trademark chuckles, low and lazy.

"For good, I hope. So long as the local authorities leave me alone." There was a pause as William waited for Hank to laugh. "That was a *joke*, by the way, about the authorities. I'm all straight now."

"Great," Hank with fake enthusiasm. "No, really. It's great to hear that. We should get together sometime—"

"I had the same thought, Hanky J! You know it's almost April. Dad's, um, anniversary? We gotta be there for Mom. But you and me, we should have a drink in the old man's honor, on our own, don't you think?"

"Sure."

"How's about today then? Meet me at the Boone Saloon. Around ten?"

"Ten a.m.? For a drink? Are they even open that early?"

"Hey, I got a busy schedule, bro. And I'm buddies with the bartender, so he'll open early for us. Plus, I wanna *see* ya. It's been a while."

Hank blinked and dropped his hand from his forehead. "Six years, William."

"There you go," William chuckled. "And when you gonna call me Billy J like everyone else does?"

Hank sighed. "See you at ten, William."

"Sounds great, Hanky—"

Hank killed the call before William could say anything more.

He stared at the phone until the screen went dark, and then all he could see was his own face reflected in it. His image looked blurry and faint in the weak light, but his eyes gleamed brightly back at him.

Pocketing his phone, he jogged back to his office for his coat. He pulled up short when he saw all the phones still spread out on his desk next to his file folders. He straightened up his files and slid them into his desk, then he gathered up all the phones and carried them into Marly's office. Their prospective clients calling in with their questions and their needs would just have to wait.

Before he left the building, Hank returned to his darkened office and pulled open the bottom drawer of his desk. He'd left it in here Wednesday night, when they got back from South Carolina.

He knew that if he was going to see Billy J again, though, he'd want to bring along his gun. Just in case.

Chapter Twelve

It was so easy to trick people who didn't have kids, Marly thought as she walked up the snowy sidewalk to her friend Nina's light blue, two-story house on the outskirts of Boone.

She'd told Hank that she needed to drive the kids to school this morning, and that she had a parent-teacher conference after that, which gave her a couple hours before Hank ever got suspicious. He didn't know how early school started, or how long a conference might last. She knew she had to make the most of this time away.

And so far, she had. Though she felt more than a little guilty for calling up Nina last night at home so she could pick her old friend's brain about drugs. She hadn't seen her in years. And then there was the whole Janice Slocumb phone call after that, which she'd handled so badly. Luckily Shelby was a true pro and helped her out with that.

Before she left the car, she checked the slim white MP3 recorder tucked away inside her coat pocket. It had plenty of memory for recording, and she tapped the Record button. A tiny red light began winking. She hated to record Nina against her will, but precautions were precautions.

After securing the recorder in her pocket, she hurried outside and up the snowy walk. Feeling suddenly nervous, she knocked on Nina's door and immediately jumped back at the explosion of dog barking that resulted.

She hadn't told anyone but Juan about her chat with Nina, and he'd been so exhausted by the time he'd arrived home from the office at eleven thirty last night that she doubted he even remembered their conversation. Which was fine with her, because her old friend Nina was a recovering crystal meth user.

The heavy wooden door opened, revealing a round-faced white woman with unnaturally black hair pulled back in a loose ponytail. Marly didn't recognize her at first, not having seen Nina in almost three years, despite living only a dozen miles away from her.

Nina's eyes were clear, her smile was authentic and free of any hints of meth-mouth, and the extra weight she'd put on made her look much healthier than she'd ever looked in the past.

Kids will do that to your social life, she thought.

"Watch out," Nina said from the other side of her screen door with a quick laugh. "He's a real killer."

Marly had been expecting a Great Dane-sized brute to leap out of the house when Nina opened the door, but instead she was confronted with a brown-and-white hound dog barely two feet high. She reached down to pet him only to find her hand encased in sharp white puppy teeth.

"Roger! Drop!" Nina shouted, pulling the dog away by his choke collar, but he still clung tightly to Marly's hand. "Bad dog!"

Half a minute later, after Marly and Nina were able to persuade Roger to release Marly's hand, they all moved inside out of the cold and into Nina's living. Marly wiped her wet hand on her jeans and laughed at Nina's repeated apologies. The mutt had managed to not even break the skin of her hand the whole time. And now he was rubbing fervently against her leg as she sat down on the faded blue love seat across from her old friend. She noticed that Nina had locked the heavy wooden door behind them before coming in here to sit down.

"We really need to get him fixed," Nina said, still watching Roger closely, as if expecting another attack at any moment. "He gets so excited to meet new people. I'm sorry. But hey, it's great to see you! It's been too long. Want some coffee or anything?"

"Nah, I'm good. But yeah, I'm sorry it's been so long. With the kids and work and all that, time just flies past you. I hope you've been doing all right. And Jack, too?"

Nina's face darkened. "We've been good. Well, pretty good. Just sort of laying low for a while, trying to get our debts under control. Jack had his hours cut at his job, and I just started a new nurse's aide gig at the university, at Student Health. It's fun, working with the kids and all their weird illnesses, but the pay's not the best."

Marly nodded, wondering if Nina had heard from any of the students about meth. She wished she had Hank's smooth way of interviewing people, where they just seemed to *reveal* key information about themselves and the case without him having to even try that hard.

"But that's just boring mundane stuff," Nina said, reaching over to pat Roger next to Marly, only to have him growl at her. "Tell me about you and Juan and the kids. And your mom is still living with you, right?"

"Yep," Marly said. "Which is a blessing and a curse, as you can probably imagine. The kids love having her around, and they're learning tons of Spanish from her. But she has her *opinions*, and loves to share them. And Juan is doing great, keeping everything—and everyone—running at work. We just got set up in a new office, too, finally."

"That old hotel, right? Cool location."

Nina started to reach out for Roger again, automatically, but then she remembered that he had switched sides. He was now protecting Marly from all attackers, including her.

"I heard how you guys found that teenage girl, that April Mae Something, that nobody else could find. I don't know how you keep managing to do that. They even showed Hank Johnson on CNN."

"It surprises me sometimes, too," Marly said, thinking about Bim as she scratched Roger's furry side until his back leg began to kick uncontrollably. "Which is kind of what brings me here, to be honest."

Nina's smile disappeared.

"Oh. I see."

"Please don't take offense," Marly said quickly. "We've got a couple cases that might be related to the recent meth incidents in Boone the past week or two.

"Marly," Nina said in a soft voice that made Roger growl. "I'm clean, and I've *been* clean for almost five years. You know that."

"I know. But I need you to educate me, give me a crash course in meth and the people who might be involved in this. Remember, all of this is confidential." Marly fought the urge to touch her coat pocket. "We're just talking."

"Yeah, well 'just talking' got Jack a couple nights in the Boone jail back in the day. He thought he was going to do some hard time while he was in there, and that broke something in him. He almost went back to that lifestyle, because of that asshole deputy, thinking he was gonna teach Jack a lesson."

Marly nodded, and then took the plunge.

"So, Nina. Do you know a Douglas Slocumb?"

Nina made a face and sank back into the couch, as if resigning herself to discussing her past.

"We used to get our meth from him, early on. Maybe eight or nine years ago? He was totally unprofessional, never had the right amounts, showed up late. But he got us high, and back then that was all that mattered. Last I heard, he'd gotten his act together, just like us."

"Actually, he's in jail again."

"Damn." Nina rubbed her arms, as if feeling a sudden chill pass through her small living room. "That's surprising. He's too *old* to be dealing like that anymore. He needs to grow up like the rest of us. Which reminds me..."

Marly stopped petting Roger and looked up at Nina, who was chewing on her lower lip.

"What's that?"

"This guy, a black guy, I know it sounds like a racist, prejudiced thing to say, and I hate to even bring it up, but I think it's relevant. He came up to me the other day at work, out of the blue, looking about fifteen years too old to be a student, but you never know, he could be a non-traditional type, going back to get his degree—"

Marly struggled to keep up with Nina's sudden run-on sentences, which was something her old friend only did when she was getting worked up about something big. Or when she was high. Marly had to believe it was the former, not the latter. Nina couldn't be snorting meth at nine o'clock on a Friday morning.

"—so he comes up to me, tells me he's got this great thing going, and do I want in? Turns out he wanted to sell me meth, had heard about me from some former friends of mine, and that I could start dealing like him and make some *real* cash. He looked down at my work shoes, the ones I've been wearing for a year and a half straight, and said I'd be able to wear brand-name stuff in less than a month if I played my cards right. If I started dealing meth! This dude was making me this offer right in the hallway outside the Student Health office."

Marly watched Nina closely, hating herself for doing it, but unable to stop, wondering—just for an instant—what Nina had said in response to that. Then she looked at her friend's face and knew the answer had been no.

"You think he was serious?"

Nina nodded, picking at her fingernails like she was trying to get the fade pink nail polish off them.

"That's messed up. This black guy, what'd he look like? Tall, short, facial hair? Fit or fat?"

"Tall, pretty fit, too. And he had facial hair like your boss, that Hank guy. Little mustache, tiny little chin beard. Not to say that all black guys look alike, right? I'm not trying to be racist or prejudiced, you know?"

Marly just nodded, hoping her face didn't show her surprise. This guy sounded a *lot* like Hank's younger brother, whom she'd met five or six times over the past two decades of working with the Hankster. But the brother traveled all the time, never came back to Boone except to visit, so it probably wasn't him. It made sense that Nina had never met him. It wasn't like there was only one black family in the Boone and Blowing Rock area. But Marly filed the "Hank's brother is a meth dealer" theory away, saving it for later.

"So other than this wannabe meth kingpin from Student Health," she began, glad to see Nina's smile at her description of the guy, "have you heard anything from any of your old crowd? Remember, this is all off the record. Anyone who might've known Douglas Slocumb, for starters? His wife Janice thinks he was set up, by the way, this last time."

"Don't they all," Nina responded almost immediately in a hard voice. She caught herself rubbing her lip and stopped, exhaling slowly.

Roger was now asleep on top of Marly's left foot. Her toes were nice and warm, but they were also going numb.

"There *were* some labs going up," Nina said after a long pause. "Jack heard about it from some of the guys he still plays cards with. And one of them caught fire not so long ago. Guess it was back in February, somewhere outside of town."

Marly tensed up. "Do you remember where?"

"Just off some country road, I think. I told Jack to quit asking about stuff like that, to not even discuss meth shit anymore with folks. It's a slippery slope, like our counselor said."

Marly sat back carefully, not wanting to wake Roger the attack dog. She looked over at Nina, who had her arms crossed tight against her chest as if she were freezing in her warm house.

"I'm sorry to drag up all those old bad memories," Marly began. "I know this has got to be hard for you."

Nina smiled and relaxed the tiniest bit.

"It's just hard not to beat yourself up about the past, you know? I look back on those days and feel like I was a different person. That all that abuse happened to another person. I mean, I was smoking and snorting these nasty chemicals to get high, and nothing else mattered. I'm just so glad Jack and I didn't have kids back then. We'd both be in jail for child abuse."

Marly thought of her own kids, and that was all it took. She risked waking Roger by getting up and sitting next to Nina so she could wrap her arms around her. Nina was shaking, and she resisted Marly's touch at first, and then she relaxed and leaned right into Marly.

"Thanks," Nina said a few seconds later, after she'd stopped trembling. She pulled away from Marly and gave her the crooked smile that had been her trademark look. "So are you a private eye now? Is that what they taught you in your training? Hug the suspect during the interview?"

Marly elbowed Nina in the side.

"You are *not* a suspect, Nina! You're helping me figure out this situation, so we can help other people and stop this mess from spreading." She sighed. "And no, I'm not a private eye. Still just a glorified secretary."

"I doubt that. You were always the star student in all our classes at App State. Getting papers in to the professors two or three days before they were due. Acing all the tests."

Marly laughed. "I wish. There were a couple classes I barely scraped by with a C. Like Organic Chemistry."

"Those were the days," Nina said. "And our biggest drug threat back then was getting some bad weed, or someone in the dorm tripping on acid. None of this meth stuff, making you so addicted right away you forget about classes and your family and the rest of your life..."

Marly had been nodding along with Nina's litany, but when Nina trailed off, Marly felt her pulse quicken.

"What?" she asked her.

"Oh, it's probably nothing," Nina said. "Just thinking about family, and about that article I saw at the Charlotte Observer website about your company. How it barely mentioned that Bim Mayer guy who works there."

"Yeah, Hank likes to take all the glory. We've all gotten used to that."

"No, he gave everyone on the team lots of props. But it was never clear what Bim did. It was strange. But anyway, as far as family goes, Jack and I were talking about Bim's *dad* the other day."

"Ozzy?"

"Yeah. He's not doing so well. We don't know what he's got, but Jack saw him at Lowe's the other week, and Ozzy looked almost yellow. He'd lost a lot of weight, too. And that's not all." Nina pulled away from Marly so she could face her. "You didn't hear this from me, but Jack thinks Ozzy might have something to do with this new wave of meth coming into town. It is totally just a theory, but he said there was something about the way Ozzy smelled that day. Like chemicals. And he might've been using, which would explain why he looked so bad."

"Ozzy Mayer," Marly said. "Holy crap."

"Like I said, you didn't hear it from me. I know that Ozzy's connected to just about everyone up here, and I know his history. But there's something going on up on Mayer Mountain that you and your team might want to investigate."

Marly nodded, at a loss for words. She hadn't been expecting this, and she felt a sudden chill.

"Actually," she said a long moment later. "I'll take that coffee you offered earlier, if you don't mind."

* * * * *

"It's a small world up here in the mountains," Marly said into her phone after tapping the Record button. She'd just said goodbye to Nina after promising to have her and Jack over for supper soon, and then she'd nearly ran to her Subaru. Sitting in the car, she'd listened to some of what she'd recorded on her MP3 player, but after a few seconds she erased the whole works, feeling like a dog for lying to her friend. She stuffed the recorder back into her inner coat pocket and started the car, hoping Nina wasn't looking out her window at that moment.

I'll never make it as a private investigator if I start compromising my standards now, she thought. Then she cleared her throat and drove off.

A few blocks later, needing to get all the information out of her head, she started talking into her phone once again.

"According to Nina, Bim's father is trying to be the new meth kingpin in this corner of the mountains. And someone who sounds a lot like Hank's brother is out looking for new meth dealers. So Hank's brother has to be working with—or probably *for*—Ozzy Mayer. Very strange bedfellows. And then there's Nina, who may or may not be caught up in the middle of all this. My gut tells me she's not on drugs anymore, but there was something in her eyes that tells me she just might have done some back-sliding. I've got nothing to prove that, but—"

Marly stopped talking when her phone beeped angrily at her.

After Juan spent all night working on it back home last night, he'd declared that the phone was finally clean. But he hadn't kept an eye on the battery, which was now almost dead. And Marly didn't have a charger with her; the kids had borrowed it the other day to keep their iPod running, and they hadn't given it back.

Off to the southwest of town, the heavy snow clouds chose that moment to break apart, and a brilliant shaft of light cut through the grayness of the morning to shine on the glistening white mountaintops off in the distance.

One of those could be Mayer Mountain, Marly thought.

She fought off the urge to pull off to the side of the two-lane back road so she could pinpoint the exact location. She knew from previous visits there that it was a big, hulking pile of rock with a flattened-off top that made it distinct. Its shape reminded her of Bim, in a way.

She found herself slowing down, putting off returning to the office and getting back to work. She kept thinking about how Nina thought she must've been a private eye by now.

And how much it pained Marly to have to say *No, not yet*.

Half a mile from the former Mountain Villa Motor Lodge, Marly turned into the parking lot at Greenway Baptist Church and quickly circled around.

She glanced at her phone, thinking she should call Juan and let him know where she was going. But the phone had completely died, its blank screen now reflecting the clouded-over sky. She set the now-dead phone on the passenger seat.

I'm not ready to go sit behind a desk again, she thought, gunning the engine. She turned back the way she'd came, aiming for the highway that led to Mayer Mountain.

I've got at least one more interview to do. This time with a certain Ozzy Mayer.

Chapter Thirteen

Big case or no big case, Bim assumed that everybody from work knew that Fridays were his day to sleep in.

And today of all days—after all that went down yesterday, topped off by that short and ugly phone call with Dad at the end of it—he really needed to sleep in. But some impossibly rude person was knocking on his front door, and wouldn't give up. Which of course meant it *had* to be Hanky J.

Fine, Bim thought. Hanky J's just gonna have to pick the lock again and come get me. Bim didn't really care that his old buddy had come and picked him up at the new office late last night, after Bim's disastrous call with Dad, saving Bim the cost of a taxi—or the pain of a cold walk back in his flip-flops—back to his apartment. Bim just wanted to sleep in for a few more hours.

But instead of the click of the lock and the creak of the door as it opened, Bim only heard one ongoing sound: the rap of knuckles on his door. He covered his head with his pillow, but the sound didn't go away.

And inside his head, he heard something else altogether, something he couldn't banish from his memory.

Dad's voice.

"Why can't you be a man and think for yourself, for once?" Dad had said in his raspy voice the instant he found out that Mom had been prodding Bim to call him for weeks. "She's just using you to get to me. Can't you see that?"

Bim had asked Dad why Mom was living down in Lenoir instead of with him up at the house. While Mom had wanted Bim to call Dad to check on how Dad was doing, Bim was actually much more concerned about Mom's situation and her well-being. Dad knew how to take care of himself. He'd certainly made that his top priority all the years Bim had known him.

"She needed some time away," Dad had finally admitted, and then coughed loudly into the phone. "It was a mutual decision."

Which of course meant it was mostly Dad, forcing the issue.

"How long?"

"Since January. Almost two months now. Don't feel all sorry for her. She's off the mountain with her old friend Emily, so they're reliving their younger days, while I'm up here trying to keep this ranch running."

Bim was ready to end this conversation—he'd been freezing his flip-flopped toes off outside the Walgreen's for the past ten minutes—but he had promised Mom he'd ask about Dad's health. Even though he truly didn't care. When in reality he wanted to ask just one question, one he'd asked Dad way too many times growing up: *Did you hit her?*

"You doing okay, Dad?" he asked instead, his voice flat and unemotional. He was so used to the gravel in Dad's voice, the harsh breaths he'd take in, the occasional wet cough, that he hardly heard them until Dad coughed again just then.

"There you go again," Dad wheezed. "Doing her bidding instead of—"

"Dad. Just... are you okay?"

There was a long pause, long enough for Bim to feel a headache coming on like a pulsing wave.

"I'm fine," Dad said, followed by a wet cough. And then he laughed—a big, hearty laugh, nothing bitter about it. "You should come up some time, Bim. We can have a beer and I can show you what I've done with the place. It's been too long."

Bim's headache intensified, the pain banging at the space right behind his eyes.

"*Sure*," he said. It had been almost two years since he'd been back up on Mayer Mountain. He found himself saying the short phrase that Dad had always used with him growing up, when the younger Bim wanted to do something with his old man. "Let's *do* that, someday soon. Bye, Dad."

* * * * *

At first Bim thought his pounding headache from last night had returned, but then he opened his eyes from his doze to find that the pounding was actually coming from his front door. Whoever was out there was persistent.

He rolled heavily out of bed, already in his T-shirt and sweats, and lumbered through the apartment to the front door, kicking dirty clothes and magazines and empty food boxes out of his way.

I'm gonna give Hanky J hell about this, he thought as he turned the deadbolt and twisted the cold door knob.

But it wasn't Hanky J out there in the cold, wanting to be let in. It was Shelby Jamiston. And she did not look happy.

"Oh hell," Bim said, moving to block her view of his messy and apartment.

"I've been knocking for over ten *minutes*," she said, teeth chattering as she spoke. "I knew you had to be in there."

Bim was about to ask her how she knew, but then he saw how red her face was.

"You should've called me," he said instead.

"Your phone's still dead, and still in Juan's office."

"Oh, yeah. That's right."

After standing in the doorway a few more awkward seconds, Bim knew he had no choice but to ask her in and risk her losing all respect for him when she saw how he lived.

"You can come in," he said. "But be warned—I wasn't expecting company."

He stepped back to let her in and looked away from the slightly repulsed look on her face. He pushed take-out cartons and pizza boxes off his rickety kitchen table and offered her a seat after brushing gray cat hairs from the chair.

"The cleaning lady comes tomorrow, I swear," he said, trying to smooth down his thick, sleep-bent hair. "And my pet cat is a slob, I tell ya."

Shelby finally unzipped her jacket and stopped shivering.

"Damn," she said, shaking her head. "It feels *way* colder up here in the winter than it ever did in Charlotte."

Bim had no response to that, other than to nod and swipe crumbs off the kitchen table.

"So shouldn't you be getting ready for work?" Shelby said with a bemused smile, eyebrows lifting. "We've got kind of a lot of stuff going on there, you know."

Bim shrugged. "Not much I can do there right now."

Shelby leaned forward, looking like she wanted to pursue that line of conversation, but then she caught herself.

Bim felt mostly relieved, but a little disappointed. He *wanted* to talk to Shelby about his real role with Finders, Incorporated. How he *really* helped the team find missing folks. Something about the way she listened to him, like she actually wanted to hear what he had to say.

But Hanky J had made him vow to never tell anyone about his real ability, and usually, as much as it pained Bim to admit it, Hanky J was right about things like that.

"Okay," Shelby said, drumming her fingers on the table for a moment. "Let me get to the point, so I can leave you be. Is there a place up here called Mayer Mountain, and if so, do you have family living there?"

Her questions knocked Bim back in his chair, forcing him to lean back. The chair creaked, loudly.

"That's not the official name you'd find on a map or anything," he said, choosing his words carefully.

Be a man and think for yourself! Dad's voice reminded him in no uncertain terms. Bim cleared his throat and continued.

"But my *family* has been calling it that for generations. We're talking back before the Civil War. We own the entire mountain. If it wasn't so rocky and steep, we could've sold it years ago to developers for millions, I'm sure, but that's how the Mayer family luck runs. We're stuck with it, and it's stuck with us."

Shelby's eyes had taken on a guarded look.

"So you probably know about the fire that took place up there in February," she said. "About six weeks ago."

"*Fire*?" Bim sat up straight and gripped the sides of the table. "No, I didn't hear about that. Crap. What burned? My dad and my uncle have houses up there. They never said anything."

"Oh," Shelby said, and then, more softly, she said, "*Oh.*"

"What?"

"Well. Here's the thing. Someone I spoke with this morning thinks it was a meth house—a shack, really—that burned up on Mayer Mountain last month."

Bim's headache came back full-force.

"You sure they said *Mayer* Mountain?" he said. "And how come it never made it into the news?"

"My contact said Mayer Mountain. A ways outside Boone and past Valle Crucis, but before you get to Grandfather Mountain. Near some place called Foscoe. As for the news not picking it up, well..."

"Damn," Bim said, closing his eyes and lowering his head. "I can't believe *this* is what he's doing now. The stupid son of a bitch."

Feeling suddenly buried under boulders of humiliation, frustration, and shame, Bim barely felt a cold but soft hand touch his on the table, just for a second.

He kept his eyes closed and shook his head angrily.

"You do *not* want to get involved in this," he found himself telling Shelby. He opened his sore eyes and saw that she was listening closely, no expression on her face other than an intense fire in her blue eyes. "My dad has never held down a real job for more than three months. This is the kind of shit he does to make money. He's a schemer, a conniver. A con man. He works harder at *not* working than anyone I've ever seen."

"Would he get mixed up in making and selling meth, do you think?"

"Hell yeah, if there was some sort of profit in it for him. He has no problem tossing the baby out with the bath water, so long as he can make money off either the baby or the bath water. *Meth*. Can't believe it."

"We have to go up there," Shelby said. "But you know that, don't you?"

The heat in his apartment kicked on with a whooshing sound, and both of them jumped. Shelby gave a quick smile, and Bim tried to return it, but the echo of his father's wheezing voice inside his head made it impossible.

You should come up some time, Bim. It's been too long.

Bim nodded, and Shelby squirmed for a second in her chair, which didn't creak a bit for her.

"I'm sorry to even ask this," she said, hesitantly. "But you're not, you know, *involved* in any of this, are you? I have to ask, because he's your dad."

"Shit, he knows better than to ask *me*," Bim said, letting a bitter laugh slip out his mouth. "He and I have never been close. I moved out as soon as I could. Actually a little *earlier*—my Uncle Harry, who's a cop, took me in when I was twelve. Back when Harry and his wife still lived on Mayer Mountain. Thirty years ago now."

"Your dad's brother is a *cop*?"

"Believe it or not. But he's about as crooked as a question mark. That's how Dad's been able to stay out of jail most of his life—he did a couple years when I was younger, which was how I ended up staying with Uncle Harry in the first place. Those were good years with Dad out of the picture. But the only lesson Dad learned during his one stint in prison was to put your cop brother on your payroll. Hasn't been busted since."

"Oh man," Shelby said, and then, to Bim's relief, said no more.

"So, to answer your question, no, I'm not involved with any of Dad's meth projects. This is honestly the first I've heard of *his* involvement in it. He's kept all this on the down-low, surprisingly."

"That's what I figured."

Bim recalled his chat last night with Dad. The old man was supposed to be up in the ranch, alone. But now that he thought about it, Bim could've sworn he'd heard other people in the background. Not the loud, braying voice of Augie Shepard, or the low, low drawl of

Uncle Harry. Bim could've sworn he'd heard *unfamiliar* voices. Which meant Dad was hosting some folks that Bim didn't know, late on a Thursday night. That was not like Dad at all.

"Hey," he said to Shelby, who was starting to glance around at his messy place, which was a bad thing. "Have you checked out the other two missing old guys yet?"

"Hank and I stopped by the nursing homes where they'd been living. Got some information about them, including the fact that the shoddy nursing home had covered up Webster Ashley's disappearance for almost five *weeks*. Hank got on the phone with his friend Miranda at the *Observer* about that as soon as we left the home."

"Did he... Did he get any things from the men's rooms? Something the men used to use a lot, or had some kind of importance to them?"

Shelby gazed for a moment down at the table, with its grease stains and scratches. Bim had got it secondhand from one of his college-aged friends when the guy had graduated and moved on with his life.

"No, I don't think so," she said. "Does he *usually* do that? Doesn't seem like that great of an idea, since it's essentially evidence. Why do you ask?"

Bim nodded once to himself, and then shook his head.

I'm not about to go into my weird ability with Shelby, right now, he thought. As Hanky J would say, she doesn't need to know. It'd only freak her out, anyway.

"No reason," he muttered and pushed himself heavily up to his feet. "So we should probably get going, right?"

Shelby gave him a curious look, as if she had more questions about the objects and the old men, and then she got up from the table as well.

"You gonna get dressed?" she asked Bim, aiming one eyebrow at his gray sweats and yellow Cheerios T-shirt.

"Of course," Bim said, sliding in his bare feet across the pale green carpet until his toes found his dirty lime-green flip-flops, which were almost camouflaged against the similarly colored carpeting. He turned back to her with a tired grin. His headache, fortunately, had faded away. "All right, let's roll."

"At least get a coat."

"I'm good," Bim said, holding the front door open for her. "If you don't mind driving, I'll treat us to breakfast. There's this great coffee shop called Stick Boy just a few blocks from the office. They make a mean latte, and their bagel sandwiches and scones are out of this world."

"Well, I already had a donut..."

"You've got space for a little more, I'll bet," Bim said with a teeth-chattering laugh as she following him outside. It really *was* cold out here.

He did his best to lower himself without a huge jolt into the passenger seat of the big Crown Vic that Shelby was driving. She looked at him with a crooked smile as she started the car.

"I guess," she said at last.

"You won't regret it. We'll need our strength if we're gonna do all we're gonna do today. We'll pick up extra for Juan and Marly. Hanky J won't eat anything we bring him, I'm sure."

"Okay, you talked me into it," Shelby said as she fired up the engine, and then drove them carefully down the steep hill leading from Mossy Creek Apartments.

And my diet *officially* starts tomorrow, Bim vowed, rubbing his bare, goose-bumped arms in the passenger seat. After we close this case and take care of Dad, once and for all.

Chapter Fourteen

Even though he'd lived here most of his life, Hank Johnson had never stepped foot inside the Boone Saloon until that morning.

He walked through the glass front door with the Closed sign still facing out and nodded at the young, bearded bartender taking inventory of his endless bottles of stacked liquor behind the long bar. The twenty-something guy took a moment to nod back, and then he pointed past a dozen round tables and mismatched chairs—all of them empty—to the booths pressed against the green-painted back wall.

That was where his long-lost younger brother was enjoying a frosty mug of beer next to the world's oldest pool table. He wore an expensive-looking leather jacket over a black T-shirt along with a frayed pair of jeans, and he had his boots up on the seat across from him like he owned the place.

William didn't even bother getting up as Hank approached.

"Hanky J!" he called, sitting up and dropping his feet to the floor with a dull thunk. "Or are you going by Henry now, all formal and stuff?"

Hank paused next to the booth, not liking where he was supposed to sit. He'd have his back to most of the restaurant there. And he knew his brother had set things up this way on purpose. William had also ordered a frosty mug of beer for him, which was quickly losing its frostiness and creating a puddle around it on the scratched tabletop.

"I am not calling you 'Billy J,' *William*," he said as he dropped into the surprisingly springy seat across from his brother at last. He made sure he didn't wince at the wetness on the seat left by his little brother's boots. "That just sounds goofy. So what brings you back to town?"

"Family," William said, holding his arms wide for a moment, then grabbing his beer when Hank didn't smile. "Got a job, too."

"Do I even want to know where?"

Hank watched William closely, not expecting to hear the truth. William had aged a bit since he'd seen him last—he had more crows' feet around his eyes, which blended in with the small, diagonal scar on his right cheek. He looked thinner, almost gaunt. Unhealthy.

"Get this," William said with a laugh. "I'm a *contractor* now. In sales."

"Where?"

"A local company. Very reputable."

Hank sighed. William hadn't changed at all. Still full of it, never saying anything when he spoke.

He could have tracked down his brother's whereabouts in under five minutes, back at the Finders office. Maybe ten minutes, with Juan's help, if William had up and left the country. But Hank hadn't wanted to know. He and William had made their choices in life, and those choices hadn't included one another.

Hank knew William was sucking him in, intentionally tweaking his insatiable curiosity.

"Well, that's great. A vague sales job at some unnamed local company. Mom will be *so* proud. And glad to see you. How long *have* you been back, anyway?" he asked, unable to help himself.

William, meanwhile, was loving every minute of this. He picked up his mug of beer and clinked it against the beer that Hank hadn't even touched.

"Since early February. Drink your beer, bro."

Hank fought the urge to slap a palm onto the table. Or possibly slap it onto the lazy grin spread across William's face.

"You've been back two *months*, and you haven't even visited Mom? You dumb sh—"

"Hey, hey, hey. How do you know I haven't been by to visit her?"

"Because she either calls or texts *me* ten times a day. I think she would've let me know."

"Wow," William said, finishing off his beer. "Ten times a day? You guys might be, like, *too* close, don't you think?"

Hank sighed and eyed the full mug in front of him. A beer would really go down nicely right about now. But he didn't want to do *anything* that William wanted him to do. Never had.

"I don't initiate it," he said. "Mom's just lonely, and trying to—oh, never mind."

William's lazy laugh echoed through the mostly empty bar.

"She's trying to find you a *lady* friend, isn't she? 'Cause she wants her some *grandbabies*!"

"Yeah, yeah. It's hilarious. I'm surprised she hasn't started in on you yet, bro."

"Oh hell, that was part of why I left and stayed away."

"Yeah," Hank said, stopping himself before he said anything more about William's sudden departures and the long silences following them. Mom had been convinced on multiple occasions that he'd died, most likely shot in the middle of some bad activities. Just like Dad.

He shook his head and reached for his beer. He watched William's smile grow wider as he took a big gulp of the bitter, slightly flat lager in one long gulp. Hit the spot, and definitely necessary when talking to William.

"So it's Mom's fault you stayed away, huh?" he asked, wiping foam off his upper lip.

William looked a bit impatient now, as if this chat had turned a corner onto a road he didn't want to go down. He waved his empty mug at the bartender before speaking.

"Partly Mom. Mostly this place. Being boxed in by these mountains, freezing my ass off half the year. I had to go someplace where it doesn't snow all winter. Southern California, Arizona. I don't mind sweating so long as I can get in the AC."

The bartender plunked down a fresh mug in front of William and took away William's empty without a word. William watched the white guy walk off.

"But mostly it's the looks I get around here. That *we* get here."

Hank saw where this was headed, and instead of trying to stop him, he took another drink of his beer. The stuff really was flat, but it at least it was still cold.

"Come on," he said. "You got looks like that because you were a cop's kid. And after the shooting—"

"No." William hadn't touched his new beer yet. "It was because we're *black*. This had nothing to do with Dad being a cop, alive or dead. This was racism, Hank. People have always been suspicious of us, watching every move we make. Like we're gonna rob a place or do a drive-by, or something. It got old. Still happens, too."

"And that's why you always got in trouble in school, too," Hank said. "'Cause the teachers were picking on you, the token black kid."

William held both arms out as if to say, *There you have it*.

Hank sipped some more beer, thinking about the way the nurses had looked at him last night at the nursing home. He had to admit, there *was* some suspicion in their eyes. Before they learned who he was and what he was doing there. It was almost like they'd thought he was someone else.

Maybe they *were* really acting all prejudiced, he thought, along with everyone else in this mostly white town. And I'm just oblivious to it, because I don't have the time nor the energy to deal with it.

He shook his head, trying to focus. The beer was hitting him harder than he'd thought. He needed to eat something. He hadn't had a beer in years.

"Anyway," he said, looking up at his brother, who was watching him with a smirk on his face. "You wanted to drink a toast to Dad."

William's smirk disappeared as he grabbed his fresh mug and raised it. Hank lifted his as well, feeling surprised at how little beer was left in it.

"To the old man," William said.

"He left us too soon," Hank said, and they clinked mugs.

Hank downed the last of his beer, grimacing at the bitterness of both the drink and his memories. He hated looking backwards; he was all about the future, not the past.

"You were what, thirteen when he died?"

Hank nodded, even though he had actually just turned fourteen at the time. "And you were eight. You probably don't remember much about him, do you?"

William had finished his beer as well, and he took a quick look at the rest of the bar while he pushed both empty mugs across the table and against the wall.

Hank blinked at the sound of clinking glass, his head swimming a bit more from his beer.

"Oh, I remember a lot. How he looked so big and tough in his uniform. How he'd lift me up every time he came home from work to hug me. His laugh."

Hank nodded along at that, smiling. He hadn't thought about Dad in those kind of specific terms in a long time, but he still thought about him—and all that he represented, really—at least once or twice a day since his death thirty years ago. That was how he honored Dad's memory.

"Yeah," Hank murmured, blinking his eyes suddenly. He felt a wave of fatigue pass over him, just for a second. Or maybe it was just grief. He'd never allowed himself a chance to indulge in it like this before.

He wondered for a brief moment if William would ever come work with him. It was a crazy idea—his brother was unreliable and quick-tempered, and he'd probably tell half the town about every case he was working on—but the guy was *family*.

Hank let his mind run with that idea for a few moments. William could settle down here at last, and they could actually get to know each other again. They used to be good buddies, back in their elementary school days, despite their age differences. Hank missed those days, back when he was Hanky J and William was Billy J. Back when Billy J used to look up to his big brother, and believe every word he said, and follow him everywhere.

"Feeling all right, Hanky J?" William said now. He'd been staring at Hank for almost a minute while Hank had let his mind wander.

"Hmm," Hank responded. It was the best he could come up with. His tongue still felt dry, despite the beer. And talking really, really felt like a lot of work.

"That's what I thought," William said. His smirk and his smile were gone, replaced by an unfamiliar intensity. Hank blinked, not recognizing this side of his brother.

"Listen," William began, his voice low and hard. "I need you and your people to knock it off."

"What—"

"Shh. Just *listen*, I said. We know what you guys have been up to. You're going to cause trouble, and someone's going to get hurt. I don't want that. Nobody wants that. So just leave this alone. Once we get things perfected, we're gonna move on to the big cities. This is just a trial run here. A pilot program, as they say. We know better than to shit where we eat. So just *chill out* for another month. And nobody will get hurt."

Hank was too confused to speak. And when he did try to say something, his jaw felt like it weighed half a ton.

"What... are you... *talking* about?"

As soon as he got the words out, Hank knew. He could see it in William's eyes, even as his own vision became slightly unfocused.

"The meth stuff, bro," William said. "That's why I came back. One of my old buddies up here tracked me down. You remember Douglas Slocumb, right? Guy about your age. He used to deal to me and my buddies back when we were in high school. He tracked me down, told me about the big plan. He didn't want a part of it, but he was looking out for his old buddies. Or so he said."

"No... No way."

"So I'm in it to win it now, Hank. I have some serious debts, and I *need* the cash. And this is something that's going to pay off, big-time. But you and your little Finders, Inc. buddies have to *back off*. We got the cops in our pocket already, thanks to our good friend Deputy Harry. We don't want to have to *shoot* anyone for getting too close."

Hank was shaking his head.

No, no, no.

"There's no need for you to come digging around, okay?" William was getting mad now. "All the old folks are fine. They *like* it there! This is what they were trained for, all those years ago. Now they actually get to make stuff, instead of teaching snot-nosed rich kids how to make stuff. It's a perfect setup. And they think they're actually *helping* people, doing what they're doing. That's the beauty of it. So don't come in and fuck it all up, bro."

Hank rubbed his face, trying to focus, but his cheeks and forehead had gone numb. This was crazy. William couldn't be a part of all this. Not after being back here for less than two months. How much trouble could one grown man get into in that short of a time?

"So you and your Finders folk can just lay off. We're taking good care of them. Just let 'em go."

"Never," Hank tried to say in a loud, angry voice, but all that came out was a whisper.

Hank's eyelids felt suddenly heavy, and he kept staring over his brother's right shoulder at the green wall, between blinks that were getting longer and longer.

"Really?" William said. "Are you really saying you won't let up? *Confirm* that for me, big brother."

Hank just stared blankly at his younger brother. William had a few tiny streaks of gray in his neatly trimmed mustache, along with his triangular chin-beard.

Finally, Hank nodded. Slowly.

"Okay," William said in a disgusted tone of voice, from what sounded like thirty feet away. He leaned back in the booth, as if needing to get farther away from Hank. "Your choice."

Hank decided to let his eyes close, just for a second. His mouth was still parched even though he'd just polished off his beer.

His flat, slightly off-tasting *beer...*

His eyes flipped open.

"You..." he began, but the world swirled away from him, though. His forehead was heavy, even heavier than his eyelids. His brain told his right arm to reach under the back of his coat for his gun, to stop William right now, demand he stop this crazy plan.

But his right arm—along with the rest of his limbs—had gone out to lunch.

The last thing Hank saw was his long-lost brother, still shaking his head slowly from side to side in front of that green wall, as if William, a.k.a. Billy J, was deeply disappointed in him. Hank wanted—no, *needed*—to respond to that look, to throw that disappointment right back in his little brother's judgmental face.

I'm not the one, he wanted to shout, who's in the middle of a drug and kidnapping scheme.

But he was too dizzy to retort, as if that one spiked beer had made him a blackout drunk.

With a rushing sensation, Hank's forehead came to rest on the table. His glasses slid off his face, and his eyelids closed and refused to open again.

Chapter Fifteen

Marly was supposed to be back here over an hour ago, and Juan was not pleased about her tardiness.

Her phone was going directly into voicemail, so he knew the battery had died. He also knew that it was his fault. He was usually right there with the charger whenever a gadget got below 50%. But here he was in his new office, cold air and the occasional bit of snow blowing in through his open window, with a dozen gadgets on his desk that needed his attention.

At some point today Marly had slipped in here to get her beloved phone—probably to make some more voice memos while she played private eye. And then her phone had died on her.

Juan's lungs hurt from caving in this morning with the cigarettes. Once he'd started with the Marlboro Reds, he'd smoked four before realizing his nose and his fingertips had gone numb out there next to the lobby. They kept the flashbacks away, though. Something about inhaling fire and smoke made him focus on the task at hand instead of going back in time to the explosion in the desert that had taken big chunks out of him.

It was while he was smoking outside, with Hank fiddling around in the lobby under that ugly-ass chandelier, that he figured out how he'd safe-guard the servers from future attacks, and also how to get back at the hackers who'd done this to them. He was 99% positive he'd figured out their location; he just needed one or two more bits of data to make sure he wasn't sending a hack-bomb to a church or a school instead of the losers who'd rained chaos down on their electronics for the past day.

He'd headed back inside, ready to implement his plan, only to have the power go out on him again. But now, an hour and a half later, everything was up and running again. He was about to start tracking down Marly with some of the fancy gadgets in his desk when he heard something outside his window.

He shot out of his office and made a sharp left instead of driving toward the front entrance. He'd been waiting for this sort of thing all morning; this was the third time he'd either heard or seen someone passing by outside, too close for comfort. He knew there were apartments for college kids a block away, but this place wasn't close to a bus stop, so it couldn't be one of them.

It was either one of Bim's homeless buddies, or someone looking for trouble. He was hoping for the latter.

He hurried past Hank's office to the emergency exit. He'd left the alarm system off, tired of it going nuts every time the power flickered, so when he silently pushed open the emergency exit door, nothing happened other than a gust of icy wind and snow. Juan bounced down the four-inch drop, wincing at the crunching of his wheels on the snow.

As soon as he was outside, he stopped, listening. He heard that scuffling sound again, off to his left. Close to his office. He couldn't see his office around the exterior of Hank's office, but he could see fresh footprints working their way unsteadily away from him, as if their maker was drunk.

Juan reached into the bag on the left side of his chair and pulled out one of his few non-computerized gadgets: a police-issue Taser he'd bought off an old Army buddy. Wedging it between his right thigh and his chair, he rolled forward, going fast now because there was no other way to get across the crunchy snow without being loud. He knew that it was a dead end once you got to his office. The mountain blocked off all other exits.

When he made the turn around Hank's office, he saw him—a skinny white man in dirty and torn jeans and a too-thin camouflage sweatshirt. Standing right the hell outside Juan's office, peeking in the window. The dumb shit had earbuds in, so he never heard Juan coming until it was too late.

If you're some curious homeless dude, Juan thought as he aimed the Taser at the guy, I'll apologize later. But you should've *heeded* the damn No Trespassing signs.

With that he pulled the trigger and sent a pair of barbs attached to wires from his Taser right into the guy's exposed neck.

The guy immediately stiffened up and froze for a second, and then his arms waved madly for another couple of seconds. Then he dropped to the ground in a heap.

"Holy *shit*," Juan whispered.

He'd never tased anyone before, and it made him feel a little sick to his stomach. He *really* hoped this wasn't some random homeless guy.

He rolled closer to the unconscious guy on the ground and reached down to check his clothes. He found a wallet in the guy's jeans, and then hit paydirt in the front pockets of the hoodie: a bunch of wires and a wirecutter in one pocket, and a phone (attached to his ear buds and still playing gangsta rap until Juan pulled out the plug to the buds) and a strange little five-sided gadget in the other. Juan grabbed everything, stashed it in the bag on the left side of his chair, and plucked the two barbs from the guy's neck so he could reload the Taser.

He looked back down at the guy, whose mouth was open and slack. His breathing was heavy, almost like he was snoring. There was no way Juan was going to be able to move him. Maybe if he had an electric chair—the kind of chair he wouldn't even let Marly consider for him.

"Marly," he whispered. He was already backing his chair through the snow, away from the guy. Having essentially disarmed the snoring intruder, he'd keep an eye on him from inside his office. Juan had more important people to take care of right now.

To his relief, Bim and Shelby were just walking through the front entrance as he was bumping his way back inside the emergency exit door. They were carrying cups of coffee and bags emblazoned with the Stick Boy logo—a stick man with a chef's hat, carrying an oversized loaf bread—as if they'd just been on a date.

"Bim, get your butt over here!" Juan yelled across the lobby. "We've got an intruder!"

"What?" Bim froze his coffee cup an inch from his furry face. "But we brought *pastries*."

Juan fought the urge to scream at his co-worker. Sometimes Bim just didn't catch on fast enough.

"Get over here and look out there." Juan led them to the emergency exit and pointed. He wasn't about to mess with getting in and out of that doorway again.

Bim tromped outside, and then came back with a confused look on his face.

"Nobody's there, Juan."

"What?"

"Just a bunch of your tire tracks and someone else's footprints in the snow. And a big blob where it looked like someone was sprawled out on the ground." Bim got an eager look on his face. "Did you actually tase someone? Sweet."

"I'll explain in my office. Come on, I got a bunch of stuff off him you both need to look at."

Shelby stood under the chandelier with the bags of food and cups of coffee forgotten on the table next to her. At some point she'd slipped into Juan's office to get her tablet, and she was now tapping away madly on it.

"It should be working now," he told her, unnecessarily, as he hurried past her. He pulled out his phone to check for any messages from Marly, to no avail.

He was torn between his need to find Marly and his drive to figure out who'd hacked them and how this quickly recovering intruder was involved in it. As soon as he was back in his office, he checked out every nook and cranny to make sure the hoodie guy hadn't slipped in through the window. No one else was in here. Just his whirring servers and his desk full of virus-free tablets, phones, and laptops.

"Bim, get in here!" he called over the din of his systems. "And bring those coffees and pastries!"

Juan set the loot he'd got from the intruder onto his desk, feeling a slight pang of disgust as he thought about how he'd pulled these objects from the clothing of the unconscious man.

"What is *that*?" Bim said, arriving with the welcome odors of hot coffee and cinnamon rolls. He pointed at the five-sided device with a lidded cup of coffee.

Juan took the coffee from Bim's hand and inhaled a big sip.

"I think he used that to screw with our security alarm," Juan said as he attached a cord to the intruder's phone. "But I'm not interested in that so much as this. *Boom*. I'm in."

He'd attached the other end of the cord in the guy's phone with his laptop he always kept in his side bag on his chair. That was the laptop with the scripts and untouchable security on it (most of which was not fully legal in the United States). With the help of those scripts on the laptop, he was able to unlock the phone and download its contents in under a minute.

"I know exactly who this intruder guy is," he told Bim, who was finishing off a pastry with a mixed look of ecstasy and guilt. "Let's see who his last call was to..."

"Juan," Bim began. "Where's—"

"Oh shit," Juan said. He knew this name—it was the second-to-the-last call the guy had made (the last had been to the Finders, Inc. main number, the jerk).

Gilbert M.

But with his mind clouded by Marly's absence and Bim's heavy presence right behind him, not to mention his utter lack of sleep the past night, he couldn't focus.

"Dude," Bim said, reading over his shoulder. "That guy should be in frickin' jail. If that's who I think it is, I mean. Gilbert Menson."

"The *kidnapper*?" Shelby said from behind them both.

"That makes sense," Juan said, holding up the phone and looking at the four other calls the guy had made to the Gilbert M number. "And if he made bail, he'd be out, for a little while, at least. But surely the cops are monitoring his phone." He snapped his fingers. "Didn't you say he was a techie guy? He might know how to get around that, so he can get revenge on us for screwing up his plans for April Mae.

Or maybe he's got friends with hacker skills. I bet they're pissed that we ruined their human-trafficking schemes Scumbags!"

And I am so gonna nail his ass—and his friends' asses, too, if necessary—to the wall, Juan thought, forgetting about Bim and Shelby for a moment. He knew a dozen ways to ruin someone's life via the Internet and the phone lines, and he had all the information on Gilbert M and his buddies right here in the hoodie guy's smart phone. They thought they were so damn smart, hacking us like this, but I'll show *them* smart...

"Hey, yo, Juan," Bim was saying, shaking his bag of breakfast items at him. "Come back for a minute, okay? I know you want to go all white-hat hacker on these guys, but it can wait a little longer, I think. We've got a case we need to close, and fast."

"Yeah," Shelby said, looking down at her tablet again. "Fast is right. Another kid ended up in the hospital after snorting this new meth. Nineteen-year-old. And once the weekend kicks off—which usually happens around noon on a Friday in a college town like this—it'll just get worse."

"So Juan," Bim said, in a tone of voice that immediately set Juan's teeth on edge. "Where's Hanky J? I mean, I tried calling him, but he never answered. And what about Marly? Did everyone sleep in on us this morning? Or take the day off?"

"Damn it," Juan said, sliding the hoodie guy's phone into the bag on his chair, followed by his laptop. He rubbed his face and closed his sore eyes. In the brief darkness, he saw Marly's face, and his stomach tightened with renewed worry. She'd been gone too long.

"Hank rushed off while I was working to get the power back on. Which it is now, as you can see. You're welcome. And Marly should be back by now."

As he spoke, he pulled out his phone once more, his fingers working the small screen almost without him needing to look. He hadn't used that app in months, but it was worth a try.

"That's strange," Shelby said. "Have you tried calling her—" She stopped as soon as she caught the look Juan was giving her. "Okay, you have, of course. She seemed a bit worked up when I talked to her last night. I wonder..."

Juan had the not-quite-legal app up and running on his phone, and he typed in Marly's four-digit PIN. He had one for her and for both kids, and even one for his mother-in-law, as much as he didn't really want to create one for her. The kids carried their rectangular tracking gadgets—which was no bigger than two kid fingers—that connected via GPS to Juan's app, inside their pants pockets, while Marly carried hers inside her purse. Just as a precaution.

Shelby had called Bim over to look at something on her tablet while Juan waited for his phone to spin through the data and connect to Marly's gadget.

"That's Uncle Harry's place," Bim said in a surprised tone, pointing at Shelby's tablet. "And Dad's place is right at the top. I don't know how he convinced Harry, who's his *older* brother, to let him have the peak for his house. I guess Harry just wanted to inherit the family home when Grandpa and Granny passed away. But I don't understand..."

"Mayer Mountain?" Juan asked, still waiting on his phone. This app was not approved by any of the phone makers, and it took its sweet time working. Who knew what kind of data it was borrowing and stealing.

"Yeah," Bim said, sounding dejected. "That's where we gotta go today."

"In this weather?" Juan said, still distracted by the spinning icon on his phone. *Working, working, working.* "Good luck with—"

He stopped when the spinning icon stopped, replaced by a map with a red, flashing dot directly in the middle.

"Oh shit," he said.

"What?" Shelby and Bim said at the same time.

Juan held up his phone so they could both see the map on his phone, which he knew matched the one on Shelby's tablet.

"Guess who beat you guys to Mayer Mountain?"

Chapter Sixteen

On their way to Mayer Mountain, Shelby kept a close eye on Bim, who sat directly behind her in the back seat. In the passenger seat, Juan typed madly into his laptop, with his phone providing Internet access, and at least a dozen different windows open on his laptop screen, one of which was tracking how close they were getting to Marly. She suspected Juan was finishing up what he called his "hack-bomb" against the guys who'd done the same thing to them yesterday. She felt both proud of his skills and completely unnerved by them.

And Bim, wedged in in the back seat along with Juan's folded-up chair, was enjoying none of this.

He murmured directions whenever needed, but as they drove through the slushy streets of Boone (the temperature was well above freezing today, creeping up towards fifty degrees), his face lost all expression, and he kept his gaze focused out the window. Soon they were out of town, heading towards Valle Crucis and Grandfather Mountain. Every now and then she caught the mountain's snow-dusted, old-man profile peeking out at her, wise and calm.

She wanted to say something to Bim, get him to talk about *anything*, but she didn't know him well enough to know where to start. In her rearview mirror she caught sight of him holding a beige business card in his big hand, turning it over and over without reading it.

And anyway, what could she say to him to make things any better? *Sorry your dad turned out to be a wannabe druglord? Sorry the place where you grew up is now a prison for old folks making meth for your Dad? And sorry he's got Marly caught up in this as well?*

After a few more miles of driving, guided by Bim's directions and accompanied by just the sound of Juan's laptop keys—and the occasional slightly maniacal cackle from the corner of his mouth—they made the turn for Mayer Mountain. Shelby winced at the rattle of wet gravel against the sides of Mom's car as they drove up a private road marked Mayer Lane. She was going to have to get this old beast detailed before she gave it back.

"Follow this up for a quarter mile," Bim said as the tires for Crown Vic spun a bit while climbing the mountain. "The first right is my uncle's place."

A mix of oaks, pines, and rhododendrons hugged the narrow, almost vertical gravel lane. There were no fresh tire tracks that she could see in the muddy gravel ahead of her. Shelby wondered what they'd do if they met someone coming down. Back all way the down to the paved road again? No thanks.

Juan stopped chuckling and typing and sobered up.

"Looks like she really is up there," he said, tapping the screen to his laptop. "What was she *thinking*, coming up here by herself? Playing detective without backup..."

"Big mistake," Bim mumbled in the back seat.

The road curved to the left ahead of them in a semi-switchback, and Shelby felt a moment of panic as the Crown Vic lost purchase in a patch of mud and snow. Heading into the curve, she grabbed the gear shift on the steering wheel and threw the old car into first gear for better traction. The engine whined an angry response, but they stopped sliding.

The higher they went, the rockier and more rutted the road became. The trees thinned out, exposing what had to be some great views not just of Grandfather but Boone and the rest of the Blue Ridge. Lots of bare trees shaking their bony limbs at the well-dressed evergreens around them.

Shelby didn't have time for site-seeing, however. She was too busy keeping the car on the road and moving upwards. The wet rocks covering the road were giving way to melting snow and mud.

"There's Harry's lane." Bim's big hand appeared right next to Shelby. "Careful. His lane has always been rough."

Shelby nodded, teeth gritted, and made the turn. The engine to mom's car roared as she slid through slushy snow and hit a pair of muddy ruts.

And then she had to hit the brakes an instant later to keep from running head-on into a huge blue pickup parked right in the middle of the lane.

A skinny old man sporting a foot-long, yellowish-white beard, with a big blue baseball hat pulled low over his eyes, sat sleeping in the driver's seat of the pickup. Mouth open, neck cocked at a painful-looking angle. Shelby could imagine his snoring from where their vehicles sat, nose to nose.

Juan looked up from tracking his wife on his laptop.

"Is that guy *dead*?" he asked.

"Ugh," Bim said, already pushing open his door and struggling to squeeze out of the back. "No. It's just Augie."

"Wait," Shelby said. "Do you mean Augie *Shepherd*? Shouldn't he be out running his construction company, instead of napping up here on the mountain?"

Bim's only response was to slam his door. Shelby watched him shamble past, and then she got out after him, heart pounding. This was no coincidence, meeting Augie up here like this. She left Juan staring at his laptop screen as if he could see through it to find his absent wife.

Shelby tried to remember what Hank and Bim said their unofficial motto was. She squelched through the muddy lane after Bim in her boots, thinking hard, to no avail. To her surprise, Augie had left the pickup running, and its motor rumbled like a snoring bear on the otherwise silent mountainside. Then she remembered.

Everyone comes home safe.

That was it. Today, she thought, might be the day we put that motto to the test.

Bim yanked open the door to Augie's truck, and he pulled the old man simultaneously out of his nap and out of his truck. Shelby got there just as Augie and Bim hit the muddy, cold ground with a pair of splatting sounds.

"What're you and Dad up to, Augie?" Bim shouted in the old man's face. Bim was down on one knee, sweatpants covered in mud, and he'd lost a green flip-flop a few feet away. Augie had scuttled back away from him so his shoulders rested against his back tire.

"Take it easy, kid!" Augie shouted in a hoarse voice. "We ain't doin' nothin'! You ain't been up here in ages, and now you come back yanking folks out of their trucks in the middle of the day?"

"Where's your work crew?" Shelby said as soon as she could get between the two muddy men. "Shouldn't you be supervising them, making sure they aren't using or dealing drugs?"

Augie let out a loud, ugly laugh at that.

"Bim, your girlfriend's a hoot," he said, shaking his head as he gave Shelby a cringe-inducing once-over. "But she's a bit, um, misinformed."

"I'd like you to tell me about Douglas Slocumb," she began, but Bim cut her off.

"Does Uncle Harry know you've been on his land?" he asked the old man, glaring at Augie. She didn't know if Bim was aware she was right next to him. "He still owns it, even if he doesn't live here anymore."

Augie's narrow shoulders sagged the tiniest bit at that. He sighed, and Shelby caught a strong whiff of liquor.

"Harry don't come up here no more either," he said in a slightly petulant voice. "All that prime real estate, going to waste. Now that's criminal."

"Good thing he's got you to look after his land for him, right, Augie?"

Feeling a growing anxiety about the time, Shelby glanced back at the Crown Vic and saw Juan tapping his empty wrist as if it were a watch. He was feeling it, too.

She held up all the fingers of her right hand and mouthed the words, "Five minutes."

While Bim and Augie bickered, she slipped off down the last hundred feet of the muddy lane and found herself in front of what must have once been a magnificent mountain house with a dented tin roof: two stories with a wraparound porch and big windows opening up onto great views of the surrounding peaks. But now the light blue paint had faded to gray, and three of the windows had holes punches into them the size of baseballs, including the round attic window forty feet up. The rhododendron bushes were in the process of overtaking most of the sagging porch.

Shelby ignored the house and followed the dirt lane curving back to the left. She had a hunch she'd find the remains of a burnt-out shack behind the house, which she did. But she hadn't expected to find *four* other small shacks as well. The remaining shacks stood over a hundred feet from the house, and they were shoddily built, unpainted on the outside, and no more than twelve feet square.

Perfect little meth labs, Shelby thought, creeping closer to the burnt husk of the fifth shack, which gave off a nasty stink of chemicals and fertilizer. That shack had caught fire, but judging by its somewhat intact condition, it hadn't exploded. They were lucky that day and extinguished it in time, but not lucky enough to prevent Douglas Slocumb from witnessing it. And Douglas was now doing time for it.

After peeking in at the piles of broken and blackened glass and pools of greenish-brown glop on the floor, she left the ruined shack and hurried over to the first of the four intact structures. She pulled open the surprisingly heavy door and was hit by the eye-watering odor of ammonia.

Peering inside the shack was like being transported to a pristine laboratory. The inside of the shack had been dry-walled and painted a bright white. Shelves filled with glass beakers and bags of ingredients lined three of the walls. A wooden work bench, also painted white, ran the length of the entire back wall, and it was covered with all the evidence of meth-mixing: Bunsen burners, oversized beakers, empty containers of cold medicine, and a couple plastic bottles of Drain-O. The room only had one window, and it had a thick red and blue beach towel hung over it like a curtain. There was an unexpected neatness to the place, as if whoever worked here took a certain in pride in what he—or she—created here.

And Shelby wanted to blow the place sky-high.

She'd grabbed a lighter from the glove box of the Crown Vic earlier—Mom always said she had quit smoking years ago, but Shelby had a good nose for nicotine—and now she had it in her hand. She didn't remember pulling it out. There were some stacked papers in the corner of the workbench. All Shelby had to do was light them up and—

Her phone buzzed in her pocket, almost making her jump out of the shack.

"Hello," she said after the third buzz, once she'd regained her composure.

"You might want to get back here," Juan said. "Looks like Bim's about to sit on Augie. Can't say I blame him, but..."

"Okay," Shelby said. "But Juan, it's *true*. They're making meth back here. They've got four shacks full of ingredients and equipment. The Mayer family's in the drug business. Can we trust Bim to keep a level head up here?"

"Damn," Juan said. "I'd love to blow those shacks to the frickin' moon."

"You and me both," Shelby said. She left the shack, glad to be out in the clean air again, and started making her muddy way back to the side of the house. She kept an eye on the windows in case anyone was inside. Just like the shacks, though, the place felt deserted. "But we need to call the cops, get them involved."

"Not yet," Juan said. "Marly's up there. I don't want her around when the cops get here. We all need to be gone before then. Don't forget that Bim's uncle—his *corrupt* uncle—is a deputy in Boone. We might all end up getting shot if he shows up."

"Damn. You're right. How about we call that Charles guy? The detective from—"

Shelby turned the corner of the house only to run into Bim. He knocked the phone and lighter from her hands, and nearly knocked her to the ground as well.

"Sorry," he mumbled, holding a hand out to help her keep her balance. She held onto it while she picked her phone up out of the mud with a groan. Bim, meanwhile, picked up her lighter and stalked off toward the shacks.

"Bim," she called. "You okay? And where's Augie?"

"Juan?" Shelby said into the phone, holding it a good half a foot from her ear to keep the mud off her. "You still there?"

"Hold on," Juan said, his voice suddenly sharp. His phone made a clunking sound, as if he'd dropped it. At the same time, Shelby heard some shuffling footsteps in the muddy lane out front, followed by a loud thump.

She looked back over her shoulder to see Augie Shepherd drop to the ground after hitting the open driver's side door of Mom's car. He must've tried to make a break for it, and Juan had reached over to stop him.

"Nice one," she said into the phone, but Juan wasn't answering.

Lowering the phone, Shelby turned in time to see Bim stomp into the first of the four shacks still standing. The door slammed shut behind him.

"Oh crap," she whispered. She was too far from him to stop him, and she definitely didn't want to get any closer now. She hurried to get the house between her and the shacks.

"Hold on, Juan!" she yelled into her phone, then killed the call.

Five seconds later, Bim came charging heavily out of the shack, his other flip-flop coming free as he half-ran, half-staggered away from the now-smoking shack.

"Bim!" Shelby called, even though she knew it was pointless. "Run!"

He made it about thirty feet from the shack before it exploded. The explosion knocked him and Shelby both to the muddy ground.

The other three shacks were too close, and they immediately caught fire as well. Within fifteen seconds, they had all exploded, one after another in a deafening chain reaction.

Shelby's ears were ringing, and a toxic greenish-gray cloud was forming over the remains of the shacks.

And Bim remained face-down on the cold, muddy ground. He wasn't moving.

Chapter Seventeen

Hank woke with a series of explosions, as if his head was breaking apart.

He felt like he'd been horse-kicked in both temples, and his heart was beating three times too fast. He still had his glasses on, which was a relief, but his eyes kept wanting to unfocus and close. He was so tired that he would've gone back to sleep, but his chest, arms, and hands were filled with shooting pain from the tight bungee cords wrapped around him, securing him to a heavy wooden chair that had apparently been nailed to the floor.

Elle Macpherson in her best '80s *Sports Illustrated* swimsuit issue getup smiled at him from the dark wooden wall, along with half a dozen other pages of swimsuit and lingerie models. A broken-looking queen bed sat pushed up against one wall, and a chipped black dresser rested against the other, under a faded Huey Lewis and the News poster.

Hank could smell beer along with the musty smell of a room that's been closed up too long. And something else, too, underneath it all. A chemical odor that immediately got Hank's hackles up.

This was Bim's old bedroom. Hank had spent the night here about a dozen times when he was a kid. The sleepovers had ended before he and Bim had made it to their teens, though, because Bim was more or less living with his aunt and uncle down the road from them on Mayer Mountain.

But why the hell am I *here*? Hank thought. The last thing he remembered was meeting his brother at a back booth in the Boone Saloon. And then—nothing.

"Nice decor," a familiar voice said from behind him, "isn't it, Hanky J?"

"William," Hank said, trying to turn his head far enough to see his brother. The memories of their chat came back to him, grudgingly.

William sniffed loudly behind him, almost a snort. "You never *could* call me Billy J, could you, bro?"

"Not after you got taller than me."

Hank leaned back hard against the chair and felt something give in the wood. He flexed the muscles in his arms and legs, then relaxed them. The bungee cords were going to be a problem. A bigger problem than William, who from the sound of his voice had kept right on drinking since their meeting at the tavern.

He still couldn't see his younger brother, as if William was avoiding him for some reason. Surely the guy wasn't feeling remorse now, after all he'd done.

"You put a roofie in my drink, didn't you?" Hank said.

William sighed loudly. "I knew you wouldn't come quietly."

"Probably not the first time you've used that. Though the first time on a *guy*, I'll bet."

"You weren't going to cooperate, bro," William said with another sniff. "Just like I knew you wouldn't."

Hank struggled to remember the tail end of their conversation at the Boone Saloon. Something about William confirming that Hank and his team were determined to crack the kidnapping case, when William was telling him to just let the case go. Hank tried to reach up to rub his now-aching head, but his hands remained tight at his side. He gazed helplessly around the bedroom, searching for clues.

"William," he said. "What are we doing up here?"

Hank heard the clink of a bottle.

"You haven't figured it out yet, have you?"

William walked slowly, almost hesitantly across the hardwood floor until he was in front of Hank, a beer bottle in his hand. His eyes were painful-looking, bloodshot and watering. Standing up he looked even more gaunt than he had at the tavern. He downed the last of his beer.

Hank tried not to let his surprise at his brother's appearance and his actions show on his face.

"You got mixed up with Ozzy Mayer?" he said. Now that he thought about it, it seemed like a natural fit, even if Ozzy was a complete racist—another reason Hank's visits to this house had ended. As a kid he'd only spent the night when Ozzy was out of town, doing God knows what back in the day.

"I needed a job, and this deal was too good to pass up. Even if Ozzy is a complete asshole."

Hank kept working the bungee cords, looking for an opening. He'd missed his workout today, so this was filling in nicely, though his muscles were starting to cramp already. He waited for William to say more about his contractor job in sales at Ozzy's "local company," but William had wandered off again, out of his line of sight, probably to get another beer.

"So what were those explosions?" he asked, craning his head to first try to see out the window next to the black dresser, to no avail, and then trying to see what William was doing behind him, also without any success.

"That's the question of the day, bro. I'm dying to go see, but I gotta babysit your ass. I think I know what they were. And that means bad things for you and your friend downstairs."

Hank could feel one of the bungee cords around his chest and upper arms slipping upwards. His flexing and wriggling was paying off.

"My friend?"

William just chuckled at the question.

"William," Hank said. He'd either loosened the other cords enough, or he'd loosened himself up enough, for him to be able to see his brother sitting at Bim's old desk, head bent low over a small pile of something white, like a spilled tablespoon of lumpy sugar. Also on the desk was a collection of half a dozen beer bottles, and Hank's gun.

With a snort, William inhaled half of the white pile on the desk.

"*Damn*," Hank said. "So that's how he got you on the payroll."

William looked up at him with glazed, surprised eyes. As if he'd forgotten Hank was there.

"Don't judge, bro. Don't knock it 'til you try it."

"No thanks," Hank said quietly. He flexed his muscles in frustration, and then stopped immediately when William picked up a fresh bottle of beer and the gun.

"Don't act all holier than thou, Hanky J," William said, staggering slightly as he walked back in front of Hank. "But that's how it's *always* been, hasn't it? Saint Hank, and little Billy J the sinner. Glad I could make you look so good, man."

"That stuff's rotting your brain," Hank began, unable to prevent himself from talking about it. It seemed so logical, so easy to just stop using. But he'd never let himself become addicted to anything other than improving himself, so he didn't know otherwise.

"Let it."

William tipped the beer up and drank long, until it was gone. His eyes watered when he was done, and he tossed the empty at the wall, hard enough for it to shatter.

Hank winced and felt the bungee cord around his hands and abdomen slide up and loosen some more.

William leaned heavily against the wall, as if throwing the bottle had sapped his energy. He looked out the window, with Hank's gun in his right hand, down at his side.

"There's supposed to be an *accident*," he said, slurring his words slightly. "That's why I drove you up here in *your* car. You should've seen me dragging you outside the saloon. I was laughing at everyone on King Street, acting like you'd gotten so shit-faced at eleven in the morning that you passed out. I told 'em your wife had just left you for another man, and they all bought it. People are so damn gullible."

William shuddered suddenly, still staring out the window at the mountains around them. This room had an amazing view, including a good look at the road leading down to where Bim's uncle lived. Hank could see smoke out there.

"An *accident*?" Hank said, still squirming and flexing. He just wanted to keep William distracted and talking.

"Your fatal car crash, man! Here's the story." He pointed out the window as he spoke, looking down as if he couldn't meet Hank's eyes. "You were coming up here to check on Bim's poor, sickly father for him, and you hit that last curve—which was slick with mud—too fast. Boom, right over the side into the ravine. *Too bad they never put up that guard rail,* I'll tell everyone. A terrible accident."

William gave a hoarse, humorless laugh.

Hank had his right hand free. He used it to reach behind him to—carefully, *softly*—unhook the bungee cord from the wooden chair frame. All the other cords went slack, just enough for him to scoot straight up, until he was standing on the seat of the chair, free from all the cords.

The whole time he'd never taken his eyes off the gun in William's hand. William had finally looked away from the window, but his meth- and alcohol-addled mind couldn't seem to quite fathom why his older brother was now standing on the chair in the middle of the room.

Those few seconds were all Hank needed. With the muscle memory of months of isometric exercises at his beck and call, he leapt off the nailed-down chair at his brother.

William raised the gun like an afterthought, but Hank got both of his own hands on it before the barrel could come close to pointing at him. He twisted it out of William's hand at the same moment he crashed into him, and they both slammed into the window.

With a dull pop, William's head went through the upper window, and the whole window frame broke apart from the force of their bodies hitting it. If the window had been any taller, they both would've gone through it and landed on the cold ground twenty-five feet below.

Instead, the wall under the window kept them inside, though William's head was covered in broken glass. He slumped down to the floor as most of it fell off of him harmlessly, but a couple pieces had embedded themselves in his scalp. He swiped at the inch-long shards, breathing fast with a high-pitched whistling sound. He'd forgotten all about Hank as he turned and tried to sit up.

"It was just a terrible accident, *bro*," Hank said as he punched William right in the nose with all of his strength.

* * * * *

Within minutes he had his brother bungee-corded to the chair—William was much heavier than he looked, but Hank was still surging with adrenaline. As Hank tossed the last of William's crushed-up crystal meth out the broken window, he looked down the mountain and saw a fog of greenish smoke filling the air. It was coming from behind Harry Mayer's old house.

Hank crossed the room, his gun still in his hand, and took one last, contempt-filled look at his brother in the chair: head lolling, nose bleeding, breathing shallowly.

"Welcome back home, Billy J," Hank said, tucking his gun into the back of his pants. "I'm glad Dad's not around to see you now."

He closed the bedroom door silently behind him and headed toward the stairs. He tried to remember where the squeaky steps were, but it had been over three decades since he'd been here last. And with all the noise he and William had just made in Bim's room, it probably didn't matter much, anyway.

He slipped down the stairs with just a pair of squeaks, crossed through a messy living room that looked quite a lot like Bim's disaster zone of an apartment, and heard voices coming in the kitchen. As he tiptoed closer, the voices grew louder, but they didn't seem to be very concerned about the noise they must've heard coming from upstairs.

"Is it supposed to snow again today?" said an old man's voice. "I'd like a nice snowstorm. Just one more before the spring thaw."

Someone coughed, a loud, hacking, wet sound.

"Tired of snow," said a raspy voice when the coughing ended. That was Ozzy, Bim's dad. "I'm ready for some damn sun."

That seemed to kill the conversation for a few moments. Standing outside the doorway to the kitchen, Hank held his breath. He was tempted to pull his gun and just walk right in there with it aimed at Ozzy.

But there were innocent people in the kitchen to consider, and his three Do Nots to remember: Do not kill. Do not compromise my beliefs. Do not let my emotions get in the way.

Shooting Ozzy Mayer would betray all three.

"So are you gonna come in here and join us for lunch," Ozzy called out, "or do you need an engraved damn invitation?"

Crap, Hank thought. I need backup here. Bim was always telling me how I always let myself walk into a shitstorm, how I was always going it alone. And now here I am at Bim's old house, without him at my side.

"You're gonna pay for that window you broke up there, too, Johnson. Don't think we did hear you two fighting. Come in here and show me who won that brotherly battle. *Hanky* J or *Billy* J?"

The way Ozzy said his nickname, in his raspy, somewhat out of breath voice, goaded Hank to take a big step forward into the kitchen.

Ozzy sat at the head of the big wooden table, of course, and he looked like hell. His face had a sheen of sweat on it under his long beard and unruly mustache, and his skin had a yellowish tinge to it. He'd dropped a lot of weight—he'd never been as heavy as Bim, but he was still a big man—but it didn't look like he was following a healthy diet. He had a nasty cough, and an equally nasty hand gun resting on the table by his plate.

To Ozzy's left was an elderly woman who matched the photos from James Holhouser's wallet, though she looked a bit less coiffed now with her long white hair pulled back and her Appalachian State sweatshirt and sweatpants. To Ozzy's right, with his back to Hank, sat a balding man about the same age as Delia, wearing a faded blue track suit, and a third elderly man dressed in similarly casual clothes. All three elderly people looked at him with bemused curiosity on their lined faces.

And at the other end of the table sat a miserable-looking Marly Hernandez. While all the others had big Styrofoam containers of takeout barbecue, hush puppies, slaw, and fries in front of them, Marly's place setting was empty. Hank noticed that her purse was sitting on the floor next to Ozzy.

Hank nodded at everyone, and gave Marly a quick wink that only she could see.

So this is where she'd snuck off to, he thought, instead of going to her parent-teacher conference. Juan is not gonna be pleased about this.

"Henry Johnson," Ozzy said, starting in on him right away, not even surprised at his unexpected appearance. Nothing ever seemed to surprise Ozzy. It was like he always expected the worst.

"Looks like the cavalry's arrived," Ozzy continued. "Or should I say, the cavalry's woken up from its drunken bender. I was just explaining the situation up here to Miz Hernandez here. So what happened to your little brother?"

"He's resting," Hank said.

Ozzy laughed, completely unconcerned about his newest employee, and then coughed. The other old folks went back to chatting softly with one another, even trying to include Marly in their conversation, though she wasn't getting involved. She kept her eyes on Ozzy and Hank.

"That would explain the commotion we heard up there," Ozzy said once he was over his coughing fit. His face looked even more pale than when Hank had first seen him. He gave a good-ol-boy chuckle. "That brother of yours is one top-of-the-line goof-up, ain't he?"

Hank just shrugged at that, not taking the bait. He glanced at the three old folks, chatting and smiling as if this was a picnic. As if they *enjoyed* being captives up here on Mayer Mountain, making meth for Ozzy and the gang.

His gaze returned to Ozzy and the big handgun resting on the table next to him.

The big man noticed his preoccupation, and he touched the gun on the table with a jaundiced hand. Everybody else at the table noticed as well. The three old folks stopped talking, and Marly leaned forward. It was like he had his hand on a self-destruct button that everyone had been ignoring until now.

"Recognize that gun?" Ozzy said, grinning and chuckling again with a wheezing sound. "You *should*. I used it to shoot your old man thirty years ago."

Chapter Eighteen

The cop was maybe twenty-five years old, with light brown hair and squinty blue eyes, and his hand shook as he handed Mom the badge. He never forgot that detail. A big white man's hand, trembling as it transferred the silver-colored badge to Mom's tiny black hand.

"He went right into the house after them, ma'am," the officer was saying. "Saved my life and the others, too. I know that doesn't seem like much, but it's what happened. He died like he lived. A hero."

As soon as he heard the word "died" he backed away from the open door and into the living room, where he hid under the blanket on the couch.

Dad's dead, *he tried to tell himself, but it didn't make any sense. He burrowed deeper into the couch, wanting to hide from the world and the reality of what had happened last night while he was happily sleeping.*

It can't be true, he thought. I'm supposed to go jogging with him tomorrow. And he was going to show me how to fly fish.

Mom finally closed the door, and in a few seconds he heard the cop car drive off. Mom had held it together the whole time she'd been talking to the young, nervous cop, but now she staggered into the living room.

"Oh God," she whispered, and then she said it again in a voice that would haunt him for years. It was like a moan mixed with a scream.

He knew he needed to get up from under this blanket and go to her, to be the man of the house now—because little Billy J sure as heck wasn't going to—but he couldn't move. He huddled there, frozen, his vision swirling behind his closed eyes as his mother cried and shouted and moaned, and he didn't do a thing about it.

Dad's dead, *he thought, over and over. But the words never made him feel anything but numb.*

His vision finally stopped spinning, and when it did, decades had passed, and he was looking at a face that once may have been familiar, but many years of hard living—and something else, like an illness—had curdled it, yellowing the features. It was a hairy face, and most of the hair had turned white since the last time he'd seen the man. Bloodshot eyes, yellowed skin, crooked teeth under a shaggy mustache.

The man—Ozzy, of course *it was Ozzy, he recognized him now—was sitting at table with three other folks his age and someone else at the very end of the table. And Ozzy had his hand resting on a gun.*

* * * * *

Bim opened his eyes with a start, sucking in a raspy breath and exhaling with a barking cough. He was sprawled out on his side in the mud of Uncle Harry's back yard, and it took him a few panicked moments to figure out how he'd arrived there.

After he made the requisite mental connections—road trip, Augie Ugh Shepherd, meth shacks, Shelby's lighter, explosions—he sat up, slowly. The air stank up here, and a greenish cloud hung over the yard behind his uncle's old house. He was freezing cold in his sweat pants and T-shirt, and at some point he'd lost both flip-flops. He stared down at his muddy toes until he could breathe normally again.

Just like the young cop in his vision, his own hands were shaking as he carefully wiped a blot of mud off the business card he'd been holding in his hand. He slid the card carefully back into his wallet, then slipped his wallet back into his muddy sweat pants.

With a jolt of surprise, Bim saw that Shelby was standing over him. She had her hands on her knees as she peered down at him, shaking her head.

"You about got yourself killed, Bim."

"I know. Guess I lost my temper. Talking to Augie will do that to you. He claimed they were using the houses as chicken sheds. That they were gonna start selling eggs down at the farmer's market every Saturday morning. A liar to the end."

"So you decided to destroy all our evidence to prove him *wrong*?"

"Oh, there's still plenty of evidence," Bim said, getting slowly to his feet and watching Shelby closely. "You don't think I was trying to cover up for my dad, do—"

"What's going on out there, Shelby?" Juan called from inside Shelby's car. From where they were standing in the back yard, Juan couldn't see them. "Need me to come out and do CPR on the big man?"

"No thank you!" Bim shouted.

Juan gave a quick laugh at that from the passenger seat. "Come on, guys, let's get up there. Augie's starting to wake up."

Bim sucked in a deep breath and immediately began coughing. The air was toxic up here after the explosions. He couldn't wait to get off this mountain, but he knew they had to deal with Dad up top. If his vision from inside Hanky J's head was true, Dad was not doing well, just as Mom had said. And he and Hanky J were not alone in the house. He remembered three other white-hairs up there. They appeared to all be eating lunch together.

And someone else. Hanky J had barely glanced her way, but Bim's quick eyes had identified her.

Marly had been sitting at the end of the table, looking a bit disheveled, and not at all happy to be there along with the geriatrics.

He stopped by the side of the house so he could lean on the old building and catch his breath. The smoke was burning his lungs, and his toes were going numb. Shelby stood next to him, watching him closely in a way that made Bim squirm.

"What was on that card?" she said. "If you don't mind me asking. The one you had in your hand just now."

"It's nothing."

"No, it's something. Otherwise you wouldn't have had it out when you went to blow up those shacks. Was it something from your dad?"

Bim felt a touch of anger at that, and he walked away from her with as much dignity as he could while barefoot and covered in freezing mud.

"Was it evidence for this case?" Shelby said, trailing after him like a determined terrier.

Bim just kept walking.

"God *damn* it!" Shelby shouted in a voice so filled with anger and frustration that it stopped Bim dead in his mostly numb tracks.

He turned to see her standing with her hands fisted on her hips and her face red.

"I can't *work* like this! You and Hank and even Marly and Juan over there have been withholding information from me at every turn, and it's not just this case. It's everything. I come to the office on Wednesday and he's not there, but Marly is, and she pulls a fricking gun on me! Hank is supposed to train me, but he fobs me off onto you, and you give me a couple crumbs and send me on my way. But I *need* this job. This has to work. And now you tell me that it's nothing, no, it's nothing, and I'm just supposed to follow you up there? How do I trust *any* of you mountain folks? Because you sure as hell aren't trusting *me*."

Bim stared at her, speechless. As she spoke her voice grew louder with each word, and she moved closer to him. He kept trying to backpedal, but she wouldn't let him escape. Her eyes were fiery, and despite the anger in her words, Bim couldn't look away from her.

When they were two feet apart—with Bim feeling foolish and fat and awkward standing there in the cold mud with this intense and beautiful woman who'd just finished screaming at him—he reached into his pocket and carefully removed the card from his wallet again.

"*This*," he said, swallowing hard, "is a card that Hanky J gave to me the week we started working together. He was so excited about the new business that he'd had four thousand cards made. I think he still has at least a thousand of these suckers, twenty years later." He swallowed, and then turned the card over to show Shelby the names on the back. "And these are the names."

Shelby made as if she was going to take the card, but instead she just hovered her hand a few inches above the card.

"Those are the four people we *lost*," he said, his voice cracking on the last word. "They died before we could find them. Each time, we were close. *So* close."

Shelby looked up from the card, eyes calmer now, but still filled with intensity. She nodded at him, just a quick tip of her head.

"I'm not sure why I had it out just now, since I've got the names etched into my brain. But due to the fact that it was something that used to belong to Hanky J, and because I had it in my hand, I was able to *connect* with him."

"*Connect* with him," Shelby repeated slowly. "What do you mean?"

Oh man, Bim thought. I need to shut up, already.

He jumped as Juan hit the horn for the Crown Vic.

"Hurry up, guys!" Juan shouted.

"Hold on a sec," Shelby called. "We'll be right there."

Bim glanced over at Juan in the passenger seat of the muddy car and saw that Augie was still flat on his back next to the open driver's side door.

After all these years, Bim had never told Juan or Marly about his abilities. Only Hanky J knew.

Sorry, Hanky J, Bim thought. She needs to know.

"So," he said. "I'm trusting you with this information, Shelby."

Something cracked in her demeanor when he said this, and she gave him a crooked smile that somehow eased Bim's worries and at the same time lifted his spirits.

"Okay, so here's the deal. If I can get one or two items that belong to someone, I can usually connect with them. Mentally. I know it sounds crazy, and for a long time—especially when I was in my teens—I thought I *was* crazy, hearing voices, all that. But then, with Hanky J's help, I figured out that this really *was* a gift. Something I could do to help people. It just takes some concentration on my part. It even works when I'm asleep. So when I got knocked out just then, with Hanky J's card in my hand, I connected with *his* mind. At that moment, for some reason, he was thinking about the day his dad died, which is odd, because that was thirty damn years ago."

Shelby was nodding, eyes wide. A smile formed slowly on her face, like the sun coming up over a darkened ridge.

"So *that's* how you find the people that nobody else could find. Like April Mae."

Bim gave a shy grin and nodded.

"We had a bracelet that belonged to her. That's all we needed. Well, that and a lot of hacking and Internet searches by Juan, and half a million phone calls by Marly. Hanky J, as usual, was the closer on that deal. I think he just wanted to look that kidnapper in the eye and get him to explain why he'd do such a thing, but April Mae brained the guy with a rock the minute we got there. Tough kid. So yeah, it was kind of a group effort, rescuing her."

He knew he was babbling, but he couldn't seem to stop, even if he was freezing out here and it had to be nice and toasty inside the idling car. Shelby looked right at him, not glancing away like most women did around him. She was listening to everything he was saying.

"So that's it," she said, nodding slowly but watching him very, very carefully, as if he were setting her up for a punchline. "You're *psychic.*"

"Oh God," Bim said with a shudder. "Please don't ever, ever call me that."

Juan tooted the horn again. Bim waved at Juan to let him know they were coming, and when he looked back at Shelby, she was still gazing intently at him. One eyebrow lifted, just the tiniest bit, as if she'd made some sort of decision, or come to a kind of conclusion about all he'd said.

She probably decided, Bim thought, that I'm totally nuts.

Without a word, Shelby touched the card in Bim's left hand, her cold fingers brushing his. He tried not to jump at the contact, but he felt a jolt of energy run up his entire arm. She gazed at both sides of the card.

"There's no more room for any more names there," she said in a soft voice. "So you don't need to worry."

Bim had to grin at that. They started walking over the muddy gravel to the car.

"Thanks. And you're right. I think Hanky J has found them already, if what I saw when I connected to him just now was accurate. Three other old folks sitting at a table, with Marly at the end."

"She's okay? They're *all* okay? Thank God."

They were standing outside the idling car, next to Augie on the cold ground. The old guy was still knocked out from his contact with the car door. Bim spoke in a strained whisper as he reached down to pull and drag Augie into the back seat.

Don't tell Juan just yet, all right? About me, I mean. He doesn't know, and he'd never understand. But we'll definitely tell him about Marly."

Shelby nodded, and with Augie seat-belted into the back seat, they both got back into the blessedly warm car.

Next to the old man, Bim winced at the smell of unwashed clothes and cigarette smoke coming off of Augie next to him. He tipped the old man's face away from him so his foul breath pointed at the window instead of at him.

As Shelby backed the car out of Uncle Harry's lane and returned them to the road leading up to the Mayer ranch, Bim thought about the one person he hadn't mentioned seeing in his vision.

Dad.

The old man had looked like hell. As if he'd been doing nothing but smoking unfiltered cigarettes and drinking cheap whiskey for the past couple of years since Bim had seen him last. His skin was jaundiced and loose, like he'd lost a lot of weight, and not in a healthy way. Definitely not on purpose, knowing Dad.

"Pull over there," he said to Shelby when they were almost in sight of the house. He pointed at a barely noticeable dirt road heading off to the right, still covered in snow thanks to all the trees around it, blocking the sunlight. "We'll walk the rest of the way. Element of surprise and all that."

"Yeah," Juan said, giving Bim a disgusted look. "Piece of cake, *walking* the rest of the way. No way I can get my chair up that."

"Listen," Bim began. "Marly's up there, and she's okay. Trust me on that. We need you to stay here and keep an eye on Augie, and watch out for anyone else who might be coming up to Dad's place."

"Call my cell to warn us if they do," Shelby said. "And thanks, Juan."

"Yeah, yeah," he muttered. "You'd better be right about all this, Bim. Or I'll find a way up there to get to Marly. Even if I have to crawl on my belly through the mud and snow."

"We'll get her, and the others, too," Bim said, and then he pushed his way out of the car and back into the cold.

He caught up to Shelby, and they started walking up the last mud-and-snow-covered curve leading up to the Mayer ranch. The old wooden gate that Dad never used came into sight, along with the split-rail fence leading up to the ranch behind the gate. Bim really wished he had some boots, or at least some flip-flops.

"Okay," he said to Shelby, out of breath already. "Let's go meet my dad."

Chapter Nineteen

"*Don't*," was all that Hank could say to Bim's father. His head started spinning the instant Ozzy had made his unexpected confession, as if he'd been slipped another roofie in his drink, and it was now picking up speed. He knew that Ozzy would say anything to further his own twisted agenda. And he knew Ozzy was just trying to piss him off.

But deep down, he *also* knew that Ozzy was telling the truth. It all made sense.

"Don't," he began again, "talk about my dad. You have no right, Mr. Mayer."

Ozzy shrugged, patting the gun sitting on the table like it was an old pet he'd kept around a few years too long.

"The truth always hurts, boy, but you need to know it sooner or later. It all comes out in the end."

He began coughing at that, ten second of jagged barks that sounded much too wet to be healthy.

The instant the old man called him "boy," Hank had to fight the urge to grab for Ozzy's gun. He was only twelve feet away from him at the head of the big table, and Ozzy was sick and slow, while Hank was fit and young.

But his arms and legs now felt like lead after their flexing workout back in the chair upstairs, and all the adrenaline he'd had in him from fighting William had drained away. He felt empty and tired.

And he couldn't help himself; he needed to know what Ozzy was about to say.

"Were you in the farmhouse?" Hank said, his voice barely audible in his own ears. Nobody but the cops knew about the other guy; it hadn't been reported that anyone from inside the house had escaped. The first shooter, Benny Stillman, had been taken down by Hank's dad, before Bim's dad took *him* down. The rest had been covered up.

Ozzy gave one last, somehow proud-sounding cough. Hank saw splotchy bruises up and down Ozzy's bare, yellow-tinted forearms, as if someone had been peppering him with punches. His eyes were red and bleary-looking, but his voice remained belligerent.

"They shouldn't have come at us like that," he rasped, "guns drawn, no vests, nothing. Just the three of them, charging the house. Shooting my buddy Stillman through the window. That damn kid deputy should've taken my bullet, but Henry got between me and him. Your daddy. Took one right in the face."

"Shut up," Hank said, barely a whisper.

"From this gun right here."

"That's *enough*!" Hank shouted.

He'd been picturing the scene in his own mind's eye for three decades. He'd visited the now-abandoned farmhouse multiple times, at first looking for any trace of Dad's blood, then later, looking for some sense of why it all had to happen at this place, and what Dad had been thinking as his life just stopped.

He never knew he'd been shot in the back. Mom hadn't told him that.

"Then you ran," Hank said. "You shot him, and then you turned tail."

The corner of Ozzy's mouth twitched at that, just for an instant. But Hank had seen it.

"And your other buddies—the ones that weren't in that farmhouse—never ratted you out, even though they took the blame for the robberies. There was never any report of a second shooter, thanks your brother. Deputy Harry Mayer took care of that. He was the third cop at the scene. How he's kept his job on the force all these years, I'll never know."

"He's a good man," Ozzy said, almost defensively. "He takes care of his blood. Unlike *some* folk." Ozzy lifted his bearded jaw, aiming it in the direction of Bim's bedroom upstairs, where Hank had left William.

Hank now stood just a few feet from a grinning, wheezing Ozzy Mayer. He didn't recall crossing the kitchen toward the old man. While Ozzy rested his bruised and jaundiced hand on his gun, Hank now gripped the handle of his own gun in the back of his pants.

Ozzy made no move to lift his gun. In fact, he looked even more relaxed than he had before Hank had been summoned into his kitchen. It was as if his face-to-face talk with the son of the man he'd killed had put everything right in his world. While unmooring Hank from his own reality.

Hank gripped his own gun tighter behind his back, about to say something else to Ozzy, when he heard a tiny gasp to his right. He remembered the other four people sitting at the table. From the middle of the table, Delia Holhouser and the two older men—Blake Barham and Webster Ashley, no doubt—stared at Hank as if *he* were the convicted felon in the room, not Ozzy. He had a sudden need to apologize to them for interrupting their lunch like this, and then he stopped himself when he caught Marly's gaze at the far end of the table.

Marly nodded at him, almost imperceptibly. She lifted her right hand a few inches, just enough for Hank to see the slim white MP3 recorder in the palm of her hand. A red light winked at him as it recorded everything in the room, including Ozzy Mayer's confession to a thirty-year-old crime.

Marly's resourcefulness helped Hank pull himself together. He took a step back and exhaled, slowly. Loosened his grip on his gun.

Time to take a different approach, he thought. If I keep talking to Ozzy, I'll just end up shooting him.

"Mrs. Holhouser," he said to the woman next to Ozzy. "Aren't you ready to go home?"

Delia gave him a confused look. "Why would I want to do that?"

"Well," Hank said, surprised by her immediate response. She looked clear-eyes and sober, so he knew she wasn't under the influence or having a senior moment. "Do you mean you'd rather stay here? Against your will?"

She shook her head and smiled. "Do I *look* like I'm here against my will?"

Hank looked at her and the other two elderly men, as if for the first time. They were relaxed but focused, like long-time colleagues taking a break but already itching to get back to work.

"He didn't kidnap you?"

All three of them laughed at that.

"Nope," said one of the men.

"Kidnapping," said the other. "Right."

Delia was shook her head and smiled.

"We can leave at any time," she said. "But this opportunity's too good to pass up. It might look like an odd set-up at first glance, but once you get over that, it's actually quite perfect for the work we're doing."

Hank was so fascinated he barely paid any attention to Ozzy on his left.

"But don't you miss your husband?"

"Billy J is going to take me by the home in a few days," she said. "Of course I miss James, but this is fascinating work. Possibly groundbreaking work. Wouldn't you agree, guys?"

She smiled over at the other two older men, and they gave hesitant nods in return. Their opinion of their work here appeared to be starting to sour, at last.

"It'd not even the prestige we might earn," Delia continued when the other men gave her their muted reactions. "It's the work itself. You don't know this, but retired life is a living hell."

The old man closest to Hank cleared his throat and nodded.

"There's nothing to do to fill your time," he said. "No meaningful activity, unless you call cleaning your house for the hundredth time this month, or doing a couple loads of laundry every other day. It's dull, repetitive... *shit*. And it's all just a waste of what little time we have left."

"Let me tell you," said the other man, "sitting around on your hands and watching your loved ones die can quickly make you feel like life is just pointless. At least up here, we might save some lives."

Hank caught Marly's gaze. She must have heard all this before, because she looked less surprised and more exasperated than anything else. But to Hank, what these old folks were saying made no sense. He wondered if they were losing their minds, or if Ozzy had pull some sort of elaborate con here.

Hank suspected the latter. No way would these former professors do anything to harm the young people they used to teach. No matter how much they hated being retired and out of their so-called meaningful activity.

"I don't get it," he said, turning back to Ozzie. "I understand you need these good people here to make it, but why in the world would you want to get into the *meth* business, Mr. Mayer?"

He refused to call him Ozzy, though he was tempted to call him by his given name, Oswald. Bim had told Hank how much his dad had hated his real name, especially after JFK back in his Ozzy's youth.

Ozzy was glaring at Hank now, as if he'd somehow let the older man down. He coughed and spat right on his own kitchen floor.

"You and my boy," Ozzy said, his voice sharp with disappointment. "You never wanted a *real* life. Where you could be a man, be your own boss." Ozzy patted his gun for emphasis with each word he said next. "And make up your own damn *rules*. Instead of following them."

I can't believe I'm having this discussion here, right now, Hank thought. I don't want to know about Ozzy Mayer's need to be free.

"Without rules," Hank said, watching Ozzy closely now, "there's just chaos. People doing whatever they want."

"Nope," Ozzy said. "That's where you're wrong." He coughed and then straightened up, like a professor starting a lecture. "Two types of people out there. The first who just wanna be told what to do and follow the rules. Like you and Bim. And the people who want to make the rules. That's me. We get to decide. You just have to chase our dust and try to catch us. This meth operation is gonna be my legacy. My last victory against you law-abiders."

"Mr. Mayer," Hank said. "You're not going to *have* any legacy. Didn't you hear those explosions earlier? That was your meth shacks blowing up down at Uncle Harry's. Your legacy is up in flames."

"The labs?" said Delia. She turned to Ozzy, reaching out her hand for him. "You told us that was just someone blasting on the next mountaintop over from here."

Ozzy shook off her hand.

"Woman," he said, his voice sharp as a blade. "Don't believe everything you're told."

Hank saw her recoil at that.

"What did he tell you to get you to come up here?" Hank asked Delia in as gentle a voice as he could manage with Ozzy so close, glaring up at him.

"Well," she said, putting a hand up to her mouth. The two older men across from her slumped in their chairs, casting dark, slightly confused looks at Ozzy. "It sounds a bit far-fetched *now*, in the bright light of day. And I guess we all should've asked more questions, early on..."

"Go on," Hank said.

"It was going to be used to reduce the damage from dementia, like my James has. It could even prevent it altogether. Just like medical marijuana made such an impact on people with vision and pain issues, we were going to help create medicinal meth. It all made sense in an out-of-left-field sort of way."

"And I'll bet he promised you all a share of the profits when it went big," Hank said. All three former professors went silent with shock at the realization of what they'd done. "But it was all a lie, wasn't it, Ozzy?"

Ozzy didn't answer, but grabbed his gun instead. Everyone at the table pushed away from him in unison, but Hank stood his ground.

Ozzy glared up at Hank with watery, bloodshot eyes.

"Even now you disappoint me, boy," he growled, and then started to cough. He nearly dropped his gun. "I tell you that I shot your damn father in the back, and you *still* aren't man enough to take me out. I gave you your chance for revenge, the motive, even. But you didn't have the balls to pull the trigger."

Ozzy picked up his gun.

Hank had his own gun out and up in half a second, the barrel inches from Ozzy's forehead. If Ozzy's gun got any higher, he'd pull the trigger. But he never got the chance to break one, possibly two, or all three of his rules. His Three Do Nots.

"Dad?" said a voice from the back door. Hank didn't dare turn away from Ozzy to look. He knew who it was.

Bim stepped into the kitchen, and Ozzy's gun wavered.

Hank didn't move a muscle.

With a wheezing cough followed by a half-strangled scream, Ozzy put his gun under his own hairy chin. He closed his eyes.

"No!" Hank shouted along with everyone else at the table, but it was too late.

Ozzy pulled the trigger.

His gun gave a deafening *click.*

Hank just stared at Ozzy, who still had his eyes shut tight.

This was the man who'd ruined his childhood. This stretched-out, sallow, bruised-up old person in front of him.

Dad would've been ashamed to see how his killer had ended up.

He turned to the doorway at last, where Bim stood covered in mud, his feet bare and bleeding, with Shelby standing wide-eyed next to him, with her own gun pointed at Ozzy.

Bim's mouth was moving, but he couldn't seem to form any words.

I almost did it, Hank told himself. I almost shot him. Point blank range.

And that would've been something he never could have lived down. No matter how badly he'd wanted to pull the trigger and rid the world of this creature.

"He's all yours, Bim," he said. Without another word, Hank Johnson walked out the back door into the unforgiving light of early afternoon.

Chapter Twenty

"You gonna eat that?"

Even though Bim was sitting in the booth across from him, Hanky J's voice sounded like it was coming from approximately a thousand miles away. From the mountaintops for all that Bim was concerned. He didn't care about the fries and the double burger coated with slaw and mustard in front of him.

His brain was still stuck up on Mayer Mountain, along with his flip-flops and his childhood.

"Bim," Hanky J called, snapping his fingers. "Come *back*, man."

Bim shook his head, unable to meet Hanky J's gaze. He went from feeling humiliated one moment to punch-the-wall angry the next. That was just like Dad. That was how he'd been for Bim's entire life. All about Ozzy and his goddamn schemes.

Bim kept seeing his dad with his own gun jammed under his chin, parting his grayish-white beard like a black shark in frothy waters.

The crazy son of a bitch had *pulled the trigger*.

Bim blinked and raised his head. He was sitting in a booth at the Come Back Shack, a burger joint in Boone just up the road from their office, though he didn't remember how he'd gotten there. On his left was a window, and outside the snow had finally stopped falling. The sun kept trying to come out from behind the clouds, but it was losing that battle. Bim knew the feeling.

He was vaguely aware of people passing by their booth on his right carrying brown paper bags of salty, greasy food, and Hanky J's faint but determined voice coming at him as if from a great distance.

That was Hanky J for you, always talking. Never giving in.

"This is *so* not on my diet, man," he was saying. "But it tastes so freakin' good. I miss burgers. And fries. And Nutella milk shakes. Holy crap."

When Bim and Shelby had walked into the house, Hanky J had been standing right in front of Dad with his gun drawn, but it was Dad who had pulled the trigger. And it was Dad who had pulled the trigger thirty years ago as well, killing Hanky J's father. He knew that now, and the knowledge was killing him.

"Dude," Bim said. "I quit."

Hanky J set down his lettuce-wrapped burger—the guy was too health-conscious to actually eat a damn bun, Bim noticed—and wiped his mouth calmly. As if he'd been waiting for this.

"Yesterday you wanted me to *fire* you, and today you're going to quit."

"Quit smirking," Bim said, his big hands fisted and ready to pound on the food-covered table. "I'm serious this time. I mean, after knowing what you know about my dad, why would you even *want* me to work with you? Us Mayer men, we're all trouble. Just a bunch of lost causes."

Hanky J loud sip of his shake and gave him a patented, slightly exasperate Hanky J look.

"Why do we do what we do, Bim?" he asked.

Bim slumped back in the booth as best he could with his belly tight against the table.

"Please don't make me go through this, not today."

"Humor me, big guy. We started doing this because we found a *need*. People were lost, and nobody was able to find them. Remember the kids we saved? Like that boy down in Florida, in the basement? We got him *out*. When nobody else could."

Bim looked at his cooling burgers and fries and felt his stomach do a lazy flip. That basement had been pretty awful. But the kid hadn't stopped talking happily in the car about seeing his momma again, all the way to the police station, the resilient little fella.

"Okay," he said. "Why *do* we do what we do?"

"Because nobody else can," Hanky J said, smacking the table triumphantly. "So if you quit on me, you're letting down all those lost people out there who need finding. Because this is the thing we're best at. It doesn't matter what happened to my dad or what your dad did. This is *us*, Bim. Finding people is our thing. No other job will work for people like us, and for Juan and Marly and most likely Shelby, too."

Bim smiled a bit at the thought of Shelby, walking up the muddy lane with him to Dad's ranch, and how they'd talked about what it was like growing up on that rocky mountaintop. How she'd laughed at his story about falling off the roof of their porch when he was fourteen. And how she'd become deadly serious as soon as they approached the back door, where they could hear raised voices.

"In a way," Hanky J said, "your dad was indirectly responsible for the Finders. On the day after my dad died, I remember finally getting up the guts to go to Mom, and we talked about doing the right thing and protecting the innocent, like Dad always did. It was on that day I decided I had to prevent bad things like this from happening to other people. And that's what I've been doing. But I need *your* help, Bim, to keep on doing this."

"Holy crap," Bim said. "Is this like some kind of ropes course or something? Are we doing some team-building right now for Finders, Inc.?"

Hanky J tried not to smile.

"Zip it and eat your lunch, big man."

"*You* can eat," Bim said. "I might hurl if I eat anything right now."

"You gotta eat. You never know when you'll get your next meal. And this is coming from a guy who only eats one meal a day. Dig in, Mr. Mayer."

Bim rubbed his sore eyes. His head had been giving him a dull ache ever since the explosions had knocked him on his butt a few hours ago.

"Hanky J," he said in low voice. "He's got cirrhosis, from a lifetime of drinking no doubt. It's terminal. He told me right after you left and before the cops got there. He's got maybe three months."

That stopped Hanky J in mid-chew.

"Damn," he said. "I'm sorry."

"Don't be," Bim said sharply.

He took a quick breath and let it out slowly.

"He *wanted* you to shoot him," he said. "He's too proud to die like this, but also too much of a chicken to actually kill himself. So that's why he was pushing you so hard, bringing up your dad and all that stuff in the past. He wanted *you* to pull the trigger."

Hanky J rubbed his chin beard, remembering the whole thing down to the last detail, no doubt. Bim would expect no less of his partner.

"I think you're right. Damn. That Ozzy Mayer, he's a quick study. Always ready to take advantage of a situation."

"You're telling *me*?" Bim said with a humorless chuckle. "And now he's gonna die in prison." Bim waved a big hand in front of his face, as if trying to clear the air of that thought. "Let me ask you this. How did you know his gun wasn't loaded?"

Hanky J blinked a couple times at that.

"Um, I *didn't*."

Bim just stared at Hanky J, a new layer of respect for the guy getting added to his admiration of him. Crazy, brave bastard.

"Okay," Bim said.

Hanky J paused in the middle of digging more fries from the grease-stained bag in front of him.

"Okay what?" he said.

Bim finally picked up his first burger.

"*Okay*, I'll keep on working for you," Bim said, balancing the burger in his hand, mouth watering. "Just for a little bit longer, at least. Until something better comes along."

"Perfect," Hanky J said. He reached for his shake, and they toasted to it, Bim's burger to Hanky J's shake.

"My diet starts tomorrow, by the way," Bim said, and not for the first time.

But this time, he thought, will be the *last* time I say it.

Then he took a huge, Bim-sized bite from his hamburger.

* * * * *

Half an hour and a half dozen burgers later, Hank was holding his belly with one hand and steering through town with the other. He'd eaten too much, but it had been worth it to get Bim talking again, and to get him to rescind his resignation once more.

Plopped on the passenger seat, Bim was working on the last of his milk shake and squinting out through the dirty windshield as the bright late-afternoon world passed them by. Or maybe *they* were passing by the world. It was all a matter of perspective.

"So where did the old folks go?" Bim asked, chewing on his straw. "Delia and the other two old men? I was too busy dealing with Dad and the cops to notice where they ended up. And I was in a bit of a state to notice too much, as you probably noticed."

Hank nodded. "A bit of a state" was a "bit of an understatement."

"Marly and Juan took the two old men back to Blake Barham's nursing homes, since Webster Ashley's place was such a dump run by questionable folks. And Shelby took Delia to see James at his old folks home. They all had been acting like they were under some sort of spell while they were at your dad's ranch, but when they heard that gun click under Ozzy's chin, they woke up. *Fast*. They'll need to answer some questions from the Sheriff's office about their actions up there, but the contracts Marly found that were all about producing medical meth that Ozzy had them sign will clear them, no doubt."

Bim shrugged, as if it wasn't really anything, but he wasn't fooling Hank.

"That's Dad for you. His plans always *sound* like the best ideas ever, until you slow down enough to examine them, and realize that they're just hot air and mirrors."

"*Smoke* and mirrors, you mean," Hank said, grinning.

"No," Bim said, not cracking a smile. He turned away from Hank to look out the passenger window. "Hot air. Trust me on this. He's my dad."

"You okay with him doing time for all this, buddy?"

Bim slumped forward in the passenger seat as he thought about this. At last, he nodded.

"He doesn't *have* much," he said. "Time, that is. He made his choices about how he's going to spend his last few weeks. I have to be okay with it."

Hank was silent for a few long, awkward moments after that.

"Hey," he said, when he couldn't stand the silence any longer. "Guess what? I think I know why you couldn't get in touch with Delia the past few days, whenever you'd try to connect to her."

Bim turned away from the window, and Hank saw with relief that the light was returning to the big man's blue eyes.

"Really? Do tell, boss."

"All the other folks you've connected with have been missing, right? But not *just* missing. They were someplace against their will, either abducted or lost or regretting having run away from home. In any case, they were dying to be found. It was all they could think about."

Bim looked over at Hank with his bushy eyebrows raised high enough to appear painful.

"Go on," he said."

"I honestly think," Hank said, "that Delia and Blake Barham and the other old guy, Webster Ashley, didn't *want* to found. They truly thought they were doing something incredibly important up there on the mountain, the poor deluded chemists. So there was no emotional connection for you to lock onto, with your secret superpower."

"Hmm. Maybe." Bim chuckled. "My secret superpower, huh?"

Hank bit his lip, not wanting to interrupt his old friend as Bim contemplated that.

They'd both been through the wringer today, and they both had a lot to process. Hank had to decide how much to tell Mom, for one. And how much trouble he was going to allow his brother to get into as well. Right now it was just Ozzy's word against William's when it came to William's involvement in all this, and Ozzy's word wasn't worth much more than the mud drying on the side of Hank's Escort.

Also, when the cops had gone upstairs to bring William down, Bim's old bedroom had been empty. Billy J had gotten away.

"Your dad was going to teach you how to fly fish," Bim said at last, just as they were approaching the former Mountain Villa Motor Lodge.

Hank jumped at that, almost losing control of the car. Luckily all the snow had melted from the roads, so they didn't slide a bit.

"How did you—"

But he knew how Bim knew, of course. For some reason, Bim had connected to him.

"Why were you trying to find *me* by getting inside *my* head?"

"Wasn't intentional. I got knocked out a little bit when I blew up those outdoor meth labs, and I had that card you gave me in my hand. It just happened. I didn't mean to, dude. Sorry."

Hank shook his head, feeling a shudder run through him at the thought of Bim eavesdropping in his mind.

Maybe at the time, he thought, I really was lost. If I was thinking about Dad, I probably was. Good thing Bim found me. Just like the motto for Finders, Inc.

Everyone comes home safe.

"No need to apologize," Hank said. "Just don't frickin' do it again, all right?"

They were climbing above town now, winding their way up to their headquarters at last.

"Whoa! Look at *that*!" Bim leaned forward as they drove up the snow-free entrance leading to the offices for Finders, Incorporated.

Above the glass front doors, just under the roof line, sat a new, ten-foot-wide sign. The background of the sign was matte black, and fluorescent green letters on it spelled out "Finders, Inc." Next to the letters was a glowing blue laptop with a mirrored magnifying glass on its screen, reflecting the town of Boone below them. Two small spotlights at the bottom corners of the sign lit it up perfectly in the fading daylight.

"I bet you can see that all the way across town," Bim said, chuckling.

Hank had no words. It was *perfect*.

He parked the car and nearly fell out of it, still looking up at the sign. He heard Bim clumping along behind him in the old work boots he'd snagged from his dad's house to replace his lost flip-flops.

As if they'd been watching and waiting for them, Marly, Juan, and Shelby emerged from inside.

"Check it out!" Juan called as he rolled up to them. "What do you think, boss?"

"*Wow*," was all Hank could say.

"It looks pretty good, doesn't it?" Shelby said. "Wish I could say I helped with the design, but it was all Marly."

"Juan insisted on the laptop," Marly said, nudging her husband.

"It's perfect," Hank said. He was shocked and embarrassed to feel tears trying to fill his eyes. He coughed and took off his glasses, acting like he needed to clean them. "*Thanks*."

"We all chipped in for it," Marly said. "We wanted it to be a surprise, and it came at just the right time. The electrical guys were just finishing up the spotlights when we pulled up."

"They also fixed the alarms and did some rewiring so we don't ever have to deal with it malfunctioning again," Juan said. "We're up and running again, boss."

"Did you know about this?" Hank asked Bim.

Bim grinned. "Maybe. Okay, yes, I did. It was something we all wanted to do."

"And you guys made sure that everyone made it safely back home?" Hank said, needing to change the subject before he teared up again.

"Blake and Webster are all set up," Marly said. "They were pretty shaken up by all this, especially when they heard the news about their medicinal meth hitting the streets, but I think they'll be okay."

"And Delia and James were like newlyweds again," said Shelby. "Well, until James fell asleep in his chair, right after he wrote us a check for services rendered. Delia says she's thinking about getting an apartment there at the nursing home so they can be together all the time."

"Oh, and our buddy Charles stopped by," Juan said, "looking for you two, saying he'd heard all that had happened and needed to talk." He held up a sticky note. "Almost forgot. He wanted me to give this to Shelby. It's his *phone* number."

"Toss it!" yelled Bim. "If you know what's good for you."

Shelby gave Bim a sly grin and slid the note into her jeans pocket instead. Hank had never seen Bim turn such a bright shade of red.

Shelby took pity on Bim a moment later, however, when she brandished the paper bag she'd been holding and pulled out a brand-new pair of bright yellow flip-flops.

"They were all out of lime green," she said as Bim's face went even more red. "But you probably already *knew* that, right?"

Hank shot Shelby a quick look, wondering what that last comment was supposed to mean. What had she learned about Bim in just half a week? Shelby just gave him a wink and a shrug in response, and then she turned her attention back to Bim.

"Thank you," the big guy said in a choked-up voice. "These are great."

He was already kicking off his borrowed boots to try on his new flops. Never once did Bim stop grinning, and he could barely look up at Shelby's smiling face.

"All right," Hank said, "let's get back inside and finish up for the week—"

He was interrupted by the approach of an impossibly clean white BMW. Miranda Jackson from the *Charlotte Observer* popped out of the passenger seat with a notebook in her hands.

Bim slapped him on the back.

"Good luck with that, bro," he said as the rest of the Finders, Inc. team passed under their new sign to enter the lobby.

"Hey Miranda," Hank said, trying to muster up some enthusiasm. He'd forgotten all about their date tonight. "I thought we were meeting down in Charlotte, not up here."

"I got a tip about a big meth bust up here. I nearly drove off the *road* getting here in time. What do you know, Johnson? You guys still open, or have you shut down for the weekend?"

"Business before pleasure, right?" Hank gestured her toward the glass front doors of the office. "Step into my parlor, ma'am."

He took one last look at the sign above him and at all his people inside the brightly lit office. Even Bim had gone inside with the others, instead of slipping off to his outdoor office next to the pool.

Yep, Hank thought with a grin, Finders, Inc. is *definitely* open for business.

About the Author

Michael Jasper is fascinated with exploring the places where the normal meets the strange. In pursuit of this fascination, he has published ten novels, a story collection, and over six dozen short stories, along with a digital comic with artist Niki Smith. You can find more about his work at **UnWreckedPress.com**.

In the past he's tried bartending, teaching junior high, painting houses, being a secret shopper, working construction, and many more jobs; he prefers fiction writing. For his day job, he works as a technical writer. He lives with his family in North Carolina, and his website is **michaeljasper.net**.

Sign up for the UnWrecked Press Newsletter to get the latest information about the publishing company, and to get a *free* ebook filled with original stories and novel excerpts: **bit.ly/UWP-Newsletter**.